We'll Prescribe You Another Cat

Berkley titles by Syou Ishida

We'll Prescribe You a Cat
We'll Prescribe You Another Cat

We'll Prescribe You Another Cat

Syou Ishida

Translated from the Japanese by
E. Madison Shimoda

Berkley
New York

BERKLEY
An imprint of Penguin Random House LLC
1745 Broadway, New York, NY 10019
penguinrandomhouse.com

Originally published in Japan as 猫を処方いたします 2, Neko Wo Shoho
Itashimasu 2, by PHP Institute, Inc., in 2023.
Publication rights for this English edition arranged through Emily Books
Agency, Ltd., and Casanovas & Lynch Literary Agency S.L.

Interior illustrations by Alissa Levy
Book design by Alison Cnockaert

Library of Congress Cataloging-in-Publication Data

Names: Ishida, Syou, 1975- author | Shimoda, E. Madison translator
Title: We'll prescribe you another cat / Syou Ishida ; translated from the
Japanese by E. Madison Shimoda.
Other titles: 880-02 Neko o shohoì,, itashimasu.
2. English | We will prescribe you another cat
Description: New York: Berkley, 2025.
Identifiers: LCCN 2025021065 (print) | LCCN 2025021066 (ebook) |
ISBN 9780593818763 hardcover | ISBN 9780593818770 ebook
Subjects: LCSH: Cats—Fiction | Human-animal relationships—Fiction |
LCGFT: Novels
Classification: LCC PL879.4.S54 N4613 2025 (print) |
LCC PL879.4.S54 (ebook) | DDC 895.63/6—dc23/eng/20250520
LC record available at https://lccn.loc.gov/2025021065
LC ebook record available at https://lccn.loc.gov/2025021066

Printed in the United States of America
1st Printing

The authorized representative in the EU for product safety and compliance is
Penguin Random House Ireland, Morrison Chambers, 32 Nassau Street,
Dublin D02 YH68, Ireland, https://eu-contact.penguin.ie.

Kotetsu, Noelle, and Bibi

1

Kotetsu, Noelle, and Bibi

Moé Ohtani suddenly became aware that the ground beneath her was dank and soggy. She scanned her surroundings. Unknowingly, she had wandered into a dimly lit alleyway. Just a moment ago, she had been walking down the lively Kawaramachi Street. One of Kyoto's premier shopping districts, the street was always bustling with tourists and young people, and the crowds only grew larger from evening into the night. Usually, on her way back from school, Moé and her friends would join the throng, hitting up cafés and shops. But today, she was alone.

Yes, she had headed west on Takoyakushi Street to avoid the crowd but somehow ended up in an unfamiliar location. Standing in a cul-de-sac, she didn't recognize the narrow, old-fashioned block that towered before her. The door was open, revealing a hallway extending into its depths.

Where on earth . . . ?

She had been so out of it. It was precisely why she'd been called unreliable and accident-prone. Still, this was the first time she'd actually gotten *lost* because she had been distracted. She let out a deep sigh.

The best way to avoid seeing her boyfriend would be to wander around a bit. She could go to a friend's place, whine and fuss, and act like she hadn't noticed anything. She'd ignore her phone. Yes, she could continue to be oblivious. Would that delay the breakup? Or would he end things anyway with a text? It would probably hurt less that way.

She stood still, eyes fixed on the gloomy building. If only her situation would change while she stood right here in this shadowy alley. If only some higher power could flick a magic wand to prevent the impending breakup. Anything would do. She wanted to run away from it all, to look the other way. But her pointless time-wasting only amplified the pain.

For the first time in a while, she was about to see her boyfriend, but the thought brought no joy. If anything, she almost wished it wouldn't happen. She sniffled and turned her back to the building.

Just then, a small voice called out, "Hey, you there!"

She spun around, but there was no one in sight. "Hey!" the voice called again.

It was coming from somewhere above her head. There was an open window on the fourth or fifth floor. Quite high up. To her surprise, she spotted someone peering out.

"Over here!"

It was hard to see clearly against the backlight, but it sounded like a man. His voice was nasal and high-pitched; he seemed to be wearing something white.

She held her breath as she watched him hang his entire upper body out of the window.

"Be careful! That looks dangerous!"

"No, no, I'm not a dangerous person. I'm a good person."

She couldn't make out his expression, but he seemed to be laughing.

The man's cadent Kyoto accent drifted down. "Since you've made it all this way, please come up. I'm on the top floor, the second unit from the back. Don't hesitate."

"N-not at all. I'm not hesitating—"

"Shall I come down to you? It's a bit of a stretch, but

it's not impossible for me to jump from this height. No, wait, it's too far. Ahh, no, actually, I think I can manage it. Let's give it a try. Nothing ventured." The man pitched forward.

"*Wait!*" Moé screamed.

She darted into the narrow building, dashed up the stairs to the top floor, then over to the second unit from the back, where she rapped on the door. Like the building, the door—metal and heavy looking—showed its age, its paint peeling off in patches. Despite her persistent knocks, there was no response. But the man's absent-minded way of speaking, his gentle Kyoto dialect that made her feel he was letting his guard down with her, had definitely beckoned her in.

She placed her hand around the doorknob and tried to turn it. Nope, it was stuck. She applied more pressure, and then suddenly, it began to yield. Using both hands, she found a solid grip on the doorknob and pulled.

As the door began to give, she peered through the crack. Unlike the musty vibes of the rest of the building, the unit within was well lit. In front of her was what looked like a reception window. *This place must be a clinic*, she thought as she craned her neck farther inside. She spotted a comfortable chair, but no one was around.

"Excuse me?" she called out.

No reply.

That man! What happened to him? Her heart raced. *He didn't actually jump, did he?* She strained her ears. *It's so quiet.* Reluctantly, she stepped back to close the door when a female voice pierced the silence.

"What's going on, Dr. Nikké?"

The voice, ringing out from the depths of the unit, was unmistakably angry.

Peering through the half-open door, Moé spotted the back of a woman in a nurse's uniform. Her hands rested on her hips.

"Going out of your way to call down to the street like that. Do you have nothing better to do? Are you feeling bored?"

"You don't have to get so mad." It was the man from earlier. "I mean, she came all the way to the entrance and was about to turn back. It's okay if I listen to her for just a bit, don't you think?"

"No, it's *not* okay. Your important patient with an appointment hasn't come by yet, but you keep letting people cut the line left and right."

"Yes . . . But he seems to be taking a long time to get here, and I don't have anything to do."

"So you *are* bored."

Still peeking around the door, Moé spotted the man. Aged about thirty, clad in a white lab coat, he sounded like a mild-mannered, kind doctor. He looked up, and their eyes met.

"Oh! Come on in." The doctor smiled, looking relieved by the interruption.

The nurse turned around to look. *What a beautiful face,* thought Moé. Her eyes were cool; her skin, a porcelain hue. She seemed slightly older than Moé—around twenty-five. Her expression, with a deeply furrowed brow, was decidedly unwelcoming.

"Um, I—"

"Please come in. Take a seat," said the doctor.

Before Moé could push open the door to the examination room, the nurse strode out, nose in the air.

Stepping inside, Moé cast a look around the sparsely furnished space—just a desk, two chairs, and a computer. Not a single piece of medical equipment in sight.

"Don't mind her. Chitose can be a bit harsh sometimes, but she has a gentle side, too. This is Nakagyō Kokoro Clinic for the Soul. As you can see, it's just the nurse and me running it, so we really aren't taking any new patients. But we'll make an exception for you since you've come this far."

Clinic for the Soul? Moé was taken aback.

"I don't have any problems that are serious enough to consult a psychiatrist."

Ignoring Moé's wide-eyed look, the doctor chuckled. "But you went out of your way to come here, didn't you?"

"I didn't come here on my own. You called me in, and I got curious."

"Some people won't even come in, even when you call out to them. But you, you came here on your own. You climbed the stairs with your own two feet; you turned the doorknob with your own hands. If you truly didn't want to, you would not have bothered. Now, let's see."

The doctor spun toward his desk and began typing on his keyboard.

Before Moé could prepare herself, the session had begun. She had never thought about seeing a psychiatrist. She hadn't even been to the mental health center at her university. She'd never for a moment felt the need to share her troubles with a third party.

"Your name and age?"

The doctor's smooth Kyoto dialect drew her in and broke down her defenses.

"Moé Ohtani. I'm almost twenty."

"What brings you in today?"

"Well . . ."

Do I look troubled? Do I look like I have problems? It was true that until moments ago, she had been brooding, but only over trivial matters. Things were a bit tough, that was all. She figured if she kept those feelings locked away in her heart, they would eventually fade away.

She was about to say everything was fine when she caught the doctor's eye. He didn't seem at all on edge; rather, he appeared ready to be entertained by a fun story. His gaze was mysterious—attentive, but it was as if he was observing her from a remove.

"I don't want to be separated from the person I love," Moé murmured.

"I see." The doctor paused. "We'll prescribe you a cat. Chitose! Please bring in the cat!" He directed his request toward the privacy curtains in the back of the room. The nurse drew back the curtain, looking displeased.

"Dr. Nikké, this cat requires special attention."

"Ahh, yes. You're absolutely right. As one would expect, you're always on top of things, Chitose. Excellent! This clinic wouldn't function without you."

"Hmph. What a lie," said the nurse, though she didn't sound entirely displeased.

She placed a pet carrier on the desk and retreated behind the curtains.

Just what is going on?

Moé sat in a daze as the doctor turned the carrier around. Through its mesh sides, Moé had a perfect view of its contents.

"Um, a *cat*?"

"Correct. This is a cat," said the doctor. He sounded proud.

Moé stooped to get a closer look.

Brown with black stripes. Large, triangular ears standing at attention. A compact face with a sharp muzzle. It was a dignified and beautiful cat.

"It's gorgeous."

"You think so? Shall we take it out?"

The doctor clicked open the carrier. The cat emerged in a smooth motion like a rolling wave. It wasn't very large, but the patterns on its coat were so striking that Moé instinctively brought her hands to her cheeks.

"*Wow.* It's leopard print. How adorable."

The leopard-print cat was sitting upright like an ornament. Its large pupils were fixed on the doctor.

"Yes, it looks like the pattern beloved by aunties of western Japan. When an auntie wears leopard print, people say it looks flashy, but it's funny how cute it is on a cat. This one is still a baby. It'll get bigger, so the auntie vibes will only grow more intense. Take this cat home for a week." The doctor brought his ear toward the cat. "Hmm? What's that?"

He dipped his face lower and touched the cat's nose to his.

"Not aunties of western Japan? Just aunties from Osaka, you say? I see. It's not right to lump all of western Japan together, is it? *So* sorry. I was wrong to do it."

It was as if they were having a conversation. When the doctor smiled, the cat slinked backward into the carrier.

"Now, please take this Osaka auntie–style cat for a week. I'll write you a prescription. Pick up what you need at the reception desk before you head out. Oh, and also . . ."

The doctor handed Moé a small slip of paper and a booklet—a simple notebook meant for keeping track of prescriptions. Moé had one just like it at home. But as she took the journal from the doctor's outstretched hand, she creased her brow. The words "Medication Record" on the cover had been crossed out with a black pen and replaced with "Cat Record," scrawled as if by a child's hand.

"Please track what the cat consumes and produces."

"Consumes . . . and, um, produces?"

"What goes in must come out—that's a basic principle. Please be meticulous about the specifics. Make sure the intake and outgo process runs smoothly."

"*Wait a second.* You're not suggesting I take this cat home, are you?"

The doctor raised his eyebrows in surprise. "That's exactly what I'm suggesting."

Moé was dumbfounded. Looking after a cat was no simple task, not something she could do on a whim.

"Nope. I can't. It's impossible."

The doctor chuckled. "Ms. Ohtani, you don't need to hold back."

"I'm not holding back. It's just . . . I'm not confident I can take care of a cat."

She hung her head in apology, but the doctor ignored her. He placed the pet carrier in her arms.

"Here you go. Now, you're officially a part of the Osaka auntie crew. Isn't that great?"

There were so many things that were not great about this. They were in Kyoto, not Osaka. And she didn't even like leopard print. But the doctor just grinned. Half dazed, Moé left the examination room with the carrier in hand. The waiting room was still empty except for the lone chair.

"Please come this way, Ms. Ohtani." A pale hand waved at her from the reception window. "I'll take your prescription now."

The process seemed much the same as in any other clinic, though a doctor wouldn't normally lure patients from a window or offer them a cat. Moé passed the piece of paper to the nurse, who handed her a weighty paper bag in return.

"These are supplies. There's also an instruction leaflet inside, which I advise you to read carefully."

The bag contained two bowls, a plastic tray, and various packets. Moé pulled out the leaflet and started reading.

"*Name: Kotetsu. Male. Four months old. Bengal. Feed a moderate amount of cat food in the morning and at night. Water bowl must always be full. Clean kitty litter*

*as needed. Will urinate two to four times a day; will defe-
cate one to two times a day. Monitor the color, odor,
shape, and volume of each excrement. To prevent urinary
tract issues, it's important for both felines and humans to
have stress-free elimination. That's all."*

She read it through multiple times, then looked over
at the nurse, who had already turned her gaze toward
other paperwork.

"'Elimination' refers to the cat's toilet habits, correct?"

"If there's anything you don't understand, please
speak to the doctor. Now, take care."

"I mean, the shape and odor—"

"Take care."

"It's referring to the cat's poop, right?"

"*Take care.*"

Resigned, Moé left the clinic, cradling the crate with
the cat inside. The walls of the old building and its endless hallway drew her back to reality. A higher power
had not flicked a magic wand to solve her problems. Instead, a doctor had prescribed her a cat.

— —

Moé lived in an apartment rented by her father so
she could attend college in Kyoto. The apartment was

spacious and elegant, with a hallway leading into an eat-in kitchen and a bedroom—a luxury for a college student living alone.

It had been three hours since she got back to her apartment. Moé couldn't tell if things were normal or potentially problematic. Perhaps the cat had not approached the litter box because something was off.

"Is something bothering you?"

Moé clutched a cushion to her chest, keeping her distance from the cat, who sat primly grooming himself.

When she had gotten home, the first thing she had considered was where she would allow the cat to roam. She couldn't risk him snacking on something disagreeable in the kitchen. So the bedroom it was, she'd decided. But as soon as she'd closed the door behind her and popped open the pet carrier, Kotetsu had darted under the bed at an ungodly speed. Dropping to her knees, she called to him while he stared back at her. His ears, sharp triangles, remained alert. At the center of each eye was a thin black streak.

Perhaps calling out is the wrong tactic. Moé filled the bowls with food and water, placed them close to the bed, then continued to watch quietly until the cat began to army-crawl out from under the bed, one paw at a time.

He devoured his food noisily and then sat.

When Moé was growing up, her grandparents had owned a cat, so she knew all about their cuteness and caprice. Their cat had been pudgy and fluffy, and whenever she'd attempted to hold him, he effortlessly slipped from her grasp. But since she hadn't actually had to look after him, she now felt more anxious than nostalgic about having a cat in her home.

According to the instruction leaflet, Kotetsu was a four-month-old Bengal. He sported a light brown coat with black stripes around his face and upper arms. He had rosettes all over his back: rich brown fur ringed with black—exactly like a leopard's spots. The glossy, short fur made the pattern pop.

She researched Bengal cats on her phone. The breed was known to be friendly and affectionate and to possess great athleticism and energy. Their fur came in shades of brown, white, and gray, with Kotetsu's coloring being the most popular. Bengals typically reached adulthood in three months, but their build and mannerisms would apparently continue to change, so Kotetsu, thirty centimeters tall when seated, was likely still maturing. That weird doctor had mentioned Kotetsu would grow bigger.

Still keeping her distance, Moé read the instruction leaflet aloud to herself. "*Will urinate two to four times a day; will defecate one to two times a day.* It's fine that he hasn't pooped yet, but I feel like he should've peed at least once." She gave the cat a thoughtful look. "Hey, Kotetsu, don't you need to go potty? Is there something wrong?"

Food and water bowls. A flimsy plastic tray that looked like something you'd find at a hardware store. And then, there was the litter. When she'd first torn open the bag, she'd been surprised. A cloud of dust had poofed into the air, revealing a jumble of uneven granules that looked like crushed cement. She'd lined the box with the litter, and that was that. She'd done what she could.

She had a vague idea of how cats eliminated waste. She recalled how, at her grandparents' house, their cat, wearing a serene expression, would sit in a box tucked away in the corner of the kitchen. Even though it was an animal, she felt it would be improper to stare while it did its business, so she never watched too closely. Kotetsu still hadn't gone near the litter box. Maybe she should have paid more attention to her grandparents' cat's bathroom habits.

"Is there not enough sand? Let me add more."

As she was about to pour extra litter into the box, her doorbell chimed. Moé jolted in surprise.

It's Ryuji. Oh no. I completely forgot.

Today was Tuesday. Not long ago, she would have been bouncing up and down with excitement while awaiting his arrival. Her boyfriend, Ryuji, worked for a real estate agency and had Wednesdays off. Like many Japanese young adults, he lived with his family, but on his days off, he would swing by Moé's and stay over. She would skip class on Wednesdays and spend the entire day with Ryuji.

This had been their routine for almost a year. But this month, citing a busy schedule, Ryuji hadn't been over to see her. Moé thought his demeanor had become chilly, too; he was distant, gave short answers, and seemed never quite to meet her eyes. She had a bad feeling about his forced laughs, which seemed to convey a hint of annoyance.

And yesterday, she'd received a brief message from him: *I need to talk to you about something, so I'll drop by your place.* There was no way that "talk" was going to be a good one. Was he tired of her? Had he even found someone else?

This was what she had been brooding about before she'd wandered into that clinic, but taking care of Kotetsu had made her forget everything. Without a moment to gather herself, she closed the bedroom door and headed toward the front door.

There was Ryuji, dressed in a suit. In lieu of his usual greeting, he gave her a sheepish wave. Even once he was inside, he seemed uneasy, and his eyes swam around the space.

A chill seemed to creep into the room. In the past, Ryuji's mere presence would fill the space with warmth. He was kind, calm, and knowledgeable—a boyfriend to be proud of.

"Do you want something to eat? Oh, you know what? There's a new Korean drama we can watch. My friend from school recommended it. Apparently, it's super funny."

"No, I'm okay. Actually, Moé, the thing I wanted to talk about—"

"There's also that new movie. You know, the one you said you wanted to see? It's already available on streaming. But the reviews are mixed. Actually, should we order pizza?"

Wanting to dispel the bad vibes, Moé chattered

away. She pretended not to see Ryuji's troubled expression. She didn't want them to break up. They were supposed to be doing fine. She had no idea why he would want to end things.

Just as Ryuji was about to speak, a loud commotion erupted from her bedroom.

"What was that?" asked Ryuji, sounding alarmed.

"It's the cat."

"Cat? You've got a cat now?"

"No, not exactly. It's a strange story. I was prescribed a cat at a clinic."

"*Prescribed a cat?* You're kidding, right?" Ryuji chuckled incredulously.

The ruckus from the bedroom continued. Moé opened the door and peered inside. She locked eyes with Kotetsu in the act of clawing at her bedsheets. His pupils widened, and he froze.

Ryuji, too, peeked through the gap in the door.

"*Wow*, that really is a cat. When did you get it?"

"It's not mine. I got it at a clinic around Rokkaku or Takoyakushi Street with a medication rec—a 'Cat Record' journal, and I was told to take it home for a week."

Ryuji looked dubious. "I don't get it. What do you mean?"

"I know it's weird, but it's true."

He didn't seem convinced. "A cat, huh? It's fine to look after it for a while, but I have a feeling you're going to get too attached."

He pushed open the door wider and went inside, crouching low as he approached the cat. Kotetsu stayed put on the bed, ready to retreat.

"That's a cool-looking cat. Like a mini leopard. Do you think he'd scratch if I touched him?"

Ryuji reached out his hand; Kotetsu leaped off the bed and trotted gracefully to the corner of the room. Ryuji leaned against the bed and observed Kotetsu in disappointment. Moé took a seat beside Ryuji and rested her head on his shoulder.

She felt grateful to that doctor. Who would've thought a cat could solve her romantic troubles? Ryuji even had a warm look in his eyes.

"He's really cute. I heard that more girls living alone are getting cats."

"Yeah, they are," she said.

Moé followed his gaze to Kotetsu. After sniffing his food and water bowls, Kotetsu moved toward the tray of kitty litter.

"Oh, maybe he's going to do his business now."

"Oh yeah?" Ryuji leaned forward to get a closer look.

Kotetsu was stepping gingerly into the litter box. He didn't crouch immediately but pawed at the litter, making a crunching sound. Perhaps he didn't like being watched or felt distracted by their presence.

Moé couldn't bring herself to suggest they leave. It crossed her mind that if they did, Ryuji might bring up the dreaded breakup talk.

"Hey, he's sitting down," whispered Ryuji.

Kotetsu lowered his haunches to the litter, tail aloft. It was hard to get a proper look, but from his fidgety movements, it looked like he was relieving himself.

Phew. What a relief.

A minute later, Kotetsu lifted his behind and then began to scratch the litter with his front paws. Moé and Ryuji edged closer for a better view.

Then came a massive sweep. Sandy dust whirled up in a burst as granules flew out of the box. Just as Moé's mind registered what was happening, Kotetsu had stretched out his forelegs and raked out even more litter. And the intensity of it all. Only moments ago, he'd been like a child playing in a sandbox; now, he was like an excavator flinging gravel in all directions. Kotetsu turned his body and bent forward, placing his hind legs on the side of the plastic box. He released one last kick, loaded with all his might. Before Ryuji could react, the litter pelted his face like a barrage of slingstones.

"*Ouch!* That hurt!"

"Eek!"

Moé darted out of the way. The floor was covered in litter. In the explosion of dust, a black missile was soaring toward Ryuji.

Is that poo—?

Ryuji frantically brushed the litter out of his hair and face, unaware of the flecks of cat feces scattered around.

———

"And so that was why your boyfriend went home with poop stuck to his head," said Reona before bursting into raucous laughter.

Between classes, the university café sunroom, which jutted out into the courtyard, was filled with students. Reona's cackle was so loud that the girls at the next table were glancing over. Moé slouched lower in her seat.

"Come on, Reona, you're laughing too much."

"I'm sorry, but it's too funny. He was covered in cat poop . . ."

Reona looked like she was going to burst into laughter again. Moé shot her a glare.

"I made sure to wipe it all off. The kitty litter was stuck to the poop, so it wasn't that bad."

"Oh, man, you got a good laugh out of it." Reona looked amused. "But hey, it all worked out. Thanks to all that, you were able to make up with your boyfriend, right?"

"Yeah, I guess . . ." Moé answered.

To Moé, who had moved to Kyoto from the countryside to attend college, Reona was her closest friend in school and to whom she had confided about her boyfriend's recent distant attitude.

The two were complete opposites when it came to their fashion sense and mannerisms. Moé preferred floaty dresses, while Reona was known for never being out of jeans. But they enjoyed each other's company immensely. The difference in their interests only widened their horizons.

"Anyway, what caused the tension between you guys? Do you have any idea?"

Moé shook her head. "None at all. We didn't fight, and it doesn't seem like he's mad at me about anything."

"Maybe he's just moody?"

"He's not like that at all. He's always been a calm guy."

Last night, after cleaning himself of the cat litter, Ryuji headed home, saying he had to work. They didn't end up having the talk, so it wasn't like they had made up. They had simply put off whatever it was that Ryuji wanted to discuss.

"Well, you showed me his picture, and he looked like a decent person. And he's quite attractive. How did you guys meet again? At a party?"

"At a student club party." A smile lit up her face. She'd had no expectations for the event and had just been hoping to expand her social circle, but upon meeting Ryuji, she found herself falling for him instantly.

"Love at first sight, huh? Can't say I've experienced that." Reona let out a strained laugh. "I'm not saying it's not valid. Looks are a part of a person, after all. But are you aware of how they might be on the inside as well?"

"Of course I am. Ryuji is kind and faithful."

"Really? You sure it's not just an afterthought because of his looks?"

Moé wasn't bothered by Reona's teasing. Ryuji was exactly her ideal, and she was unwavering about it. That was why she absolutely couldn't let him go.

She felt her spirits sink. Until now, she had always reserved Tuesday evening through Wednesday for Ryuji. Even on days he didn't come over, on the off chance that he might suddenly become free, she took the day off from school, skipping mandatory classes.

Not wanting to spend the day alone in anguish, for the first time in a while, she had gone to campus on Wednesday.

The next time Ryuji was going to come by was likely next Tuesday night. She needed to think of a solution by then. She couldn't rely on the cat again—she had only been prescribed Kotetsu for a week.

The previous night, after burying the bedroom floor in cat litter, Kotetsu had shown no remorse whatsoever. Instead, he curled his leopard-spotted body into a ball and promptly fell asleep. In resignation, Moé gathered Kotetsu's poop from the litter-scape and logged its shape in the Cat Record journal. But the poop had been scattered about, so describing it accurately proved to be a challenge.

What will my room look like when I get home today? Moé felt depressed at the thought of returning to another disaster scene. She wrapped her hands around her mug and let out a deep sigh.

"I bet cat owners struggle with keeping things tidy. I had no idea that kitty litter would scatter everywhere."

"Doesn't scatter at my house."

Reona sucked on the straw of her iced coffee, which was now mostly just ice. Moé almost missed what Reona had said because of the loud slurping noise.

"What doesn't scatter?"

"Poopy cat litter. We use a non-tracking litter for my cat."

"Wait, *what*? There are different kinds of litter?"

"Yeah. There are many types."

"*Really?* I didn't know. I mean, that litter was given to me at the clinic."

That enormous cloud of dust yesterday—it was like a bout of environmental pollution.

"What an odd story about that clinic. Where in Nakagyō Ward did you say it was?"

"I was walking down Takoyakushi Street and found it by chance. Don't change the subject. What kind of litter doesn't scatter? Where can I buy some?"

"You're desperate, aren't you? There's a large chain pet store by the subway line. Want to drop by after cla—?"

"Yes, yes, yes!"

The pet store was roughly the size of half a floor in a large supermarket and far more spacious and neater than Moé had imagined. The airy, glass-walled store had high ceilings and was well lit. What was most surprising was the range of products—the orderly rows of shelves were packed.

Seeing Moé gaping, Reona laughed.

"Isn't it like a little theme park here? They've got everything. Cat towers. Cute cat beds. You name it. And it's not only cat stuff. They've got quite a bit of stuff for dogs, too. Over there." Reona pointed at the opposite end of the store.

"Now, the litter, litter, litter."

Reona was apparently very familiar with the store, and she quickly guided them to the right shelf. Moé grimaced when she saw the display.

"I mean . . . what's with this huge selection?"

The shelves were lined with rows and rows of what looked like breakfast cereal boxes, except there was even more variety than any supermarket selection of cereal.

"Are these all cat litter? Why so many?"

"They serve different purposes. Different materials,

shapes, and even disposal methods. What's the bath-room situation like at your place, Moé?"

"It's a regular apartment affair. The toilet has a bidet function and seat warmers. I have a lavender-colored foot mat and toilet paper holder."

"No, no, no," said Reona, waving her hand before her face. "Not *your* bathroom. The cat's. Don't make me laugh."

"Oh. Well, it's a box, like a plastic tray."

"Is it a sifting litter box?"

"Sifting? Well, it's not electric?" Moé's eyes wandered. She was feeling slightly uneasy about her own lack of knowledge.

Reona chuckled. "Sifting litter boxes aren't always electric. I just mean, does it have a pull-out drawer where the waste falls? If it's like a plastic tray, it doesn't sound like it's tiered. If that's the case, it's better if you get litter that clumps."

Reona leaned forward and scrutinized the bags of litter on the shelves.

"The one we have at home can't be flushed down the toilet, but quite a few paper-based ones are flushable. Some are made from wood chips, silica crystals, and even soy pulp. Those are for cats that like to eat everything."

Reona grabbed the bags and inspected them carefully.

All Moé could do was stand. The sheer variety of kitty litter—it seemed that she had underestimated the breadth of knowledge needed to raise a cat. *Do I need to do more research? Are cats more complicated than I thought?*

Reona offered a reassuring smile.

"What do you want to do, Moé? If you're planning on keeping the cat long-term, I'd say you should experiment with various litters, but the cat's not yours, right? So, you can try to stick it out with the current litter or get the clumping kind with large granules."

"I'll try the clumping litter."

The one Reona picked had a large cat face printed on its bag. It promised odor control, clumping, and low tracking. It was made from hinoki cypress wood chips and looked like pulverized brown rice bran.

"Want to check out the cat food?"

Moé glanced at the endless food aisle and immediately felt dizzy. She decided she'd skip it for now.

It was only after paying that she took a moment to breathe.

"I had no idea there'd be this many varieties."

"Right? Cats are practically royalty. When it comes to pets, I feel like things are getting a bit over-the-top."

"I agree."

Moé was relieved that Reona felt the same way. Reona had a straight-shooting personality and was never overly obsessed about things.

"You don't talk about your cat much, Reona. I always picture cat owners as super obsessed, constantly sharing photos online."

"There are tons of people like that, but that's not really me. People who're obsessed with their cats are like—" Reona twisted her body playfully. "*How adorable is my cat? I find my cat irresistible both when it's being affectionate and when it's being standoffish.*" She straightened her posture. "But for me, my cat's just there. You get the difference?"

"Not really," said Moé.

Reona chuckled. "I just mean the cat's simply a part of the family. They're like perpetual kids. My brother was the one who first got the cat, but for some reason, the cat wouldn't warm up to my brother. Ultimately, she became my mom's cat."

"I see." Describing the cat as "Mom's cat" had a

warmth to it, Moé thought. It seemed that a cat's position was unique to each household.

Reona said she had to head to her part-time job.

"I'd love to swing by your apartment and tell you everything I know about cats, but this month, we're expecting a ton of middle-school field trip groups visiting from other prefectures. My schedule this week is packed with all-day shifts. And honestly, isn't Kyoto's yudofu a bit extravagant for these kids?"

There was an abundance of specialty boiled-tofu shops around Kyoto's tourist hot spots. Reona worked part-time at an established Japanese restaurant near Nanzen-ji Temple. When Moé first arrived in Kyoto, Reona had taken her around to famous sites like Arashiyama and Kiyomizu-dera Temple. But ever since she'd begun seeing Ryuji, their time together had dwindled to grabbing coffee after class. It had been a while since they'd gone out together like this.

When Moé got in, the apartment was silent. She imagined how dogs would make a fuss when their owners came home, but the cat who was in the bedroom with the door shut made not a peep.

Walking barefoot toward the bedroom, she began to

feel a little uneasy. *There's not even the patter of a paw. Could he have slipped out?*

Slowly, she cracked open the door.

For a second, she couldn't work out what she was looking at.

The curtains . . .

One of the lace curtains had come off the rod and was hanging limply. Shredded and riddled with holes.

"*Ahhhh.*"

Closing the bedroom door, she slumped to the floor. She had braced herself somewhat for some damage after what the cat had done to her sheets yesterday. But she never imagined he would so mercilessly destroy her curtains. In fact, they were no longer curtains—more like shreds of fabric dangling miserably.

Kotetsu, meanwhile, was sitting primly on the windowsill, looking straight at her with his large, light green eyes. If the door hadn't been completely closed, she'd never have believed the creature staring at her with such innocent eyes was the culprit.

And the floor was covered in cat litter again. Kotetsu must have used the bathroom multiple times, because there was litter in every direction. Thankfully, the poop was intact and remained within the plastic tray. There were some hardened clumps, which she assumed were pee. "Will urinate two to four times a day; will defecate one to two times a day." There were two clumps, so it looked like Kotetsu had urinated twice. It seemed that at least the cat's excretions were as planned.

But the curtains were done for. She'd need to replace them before Ryuji's next visit.

Her heart sank. *Will Ryuji come over again? And if he does, will there be any new development?* She let out a deep sigh.

With one long, sleek movement, Kotetsu jumped off the windowsill. His steps made no sound, absorbed by the rug. His body was leopard-like, with spots that trailed all the way to his hind thighs. His small and delicate face gave him a sweetness, like a baby-faced supermodel.

As Kotetsu sauntered across the bedroom, Moé looked on, captivated: he really did look like a model on a runway. He wandered around for a few moments, before circling back toward the plastic litter box. Moé started.

"Wait a second, Kotetsu. Let me put in some fresh litter for you."

She hurriedly transferred the soiled litter into a garbage

bag, scrubbed the tray with a wet wipe, and poured in the new litter. In an instant, the room was filled with the scent of hinoki cypress.

"That smells great. Kotetsu, this one's definitely better."

As she spread it out over the bottom of the tray, it had released its pleasant scent. Importantly, it wasn't dusty like the old litter. *This is so much better, thank you, Reona.* Moé wanted her to come by while she still had Kotetsu, so she could watch while her friend, so unswayed by cuteness, fell under Kotetsu's adorable charm.

⸺ ⬩ ⸺

One week later, when Moé walked back into Nakagyō Kokoro Clinic for the Soul, she found the nurse, beautiful and aloof as ever, sitting in the reception window. She glanced up briefly. "Please come in, Ms. Ohtani. The doctor is waiting for you in the examination room."

The Kyoto dialect had a unique intonation, where even seemingly clinical terms like "doctor" sounded endearingly familiar. When Moé first came to Kyoto, she didn't know if the drawn-out endings of words were due to the local accent or if people were being overly familiar with her. But now she had gotten used to the elongated cadence that was used even when addressing respected professionals.

She liked the Kyoto dialect; it was smooth like a cat.

Moé walked into the examination room as directed. The doctor, already seated and waiting, greeted her warmly.

"Hello, Ms. Ohtani. How are you feeling?"

Moé struggled to articulate her condition, as she felt neither good nor bad.

"Umm, I'm okay." She quietly placed the pet carrier containing Kotetsu on the desk.

"I see. Just okay? There's no rush. It's always slow at the beginning. You'll feel better gradually."

At the beginning? Gradually?

Moé raised her eyebrows, but the doctor was smiling.

"Did you keep a record?"

"Oh, yes."

She handed over the journal, which the doctor scrutinized, starting from day one. As she jotted down the condition of the cat's poop and pee over the week, she couldn't help but wonder what in the world she had been made to do. If it hadn't been at the behest of this psychiatric clinic, she'd have thought it was some kind of joke.

Today was Tuesday. Since last week, she and Ryuji had exchanged messages but had not seen each other in person, and the short message she received today—"I'll drop by your place, I have something to talk to you about"—made her think, *I guess the cat's not working anymore.*

"Mm-hmm, you *have* taken meticulous notes. You're a straightforward person, Ms. Ohtani. You don't cut corners, even when it's not your own cat. Some people only see things from their perspective and bend the truth to fit it."

"Bend the truth?"

Moé tilted her head, not understanding. *He must be talking about the Cat Record journal. Does he mean some people fudge the numbers on the amount of poop or meal frequency? Or maybe neglect to keep a record at all?*

The doctor was still examining the notebook, going over it with extreme care.

"It's when people unwittingly twist things so it's convenient for them. And because they're not aware they're doing it, they don't realize how they've distorted things." He scratched his nose. "Hmm, the first two days look fine, but it seems something went wrong on day three. Am I right?"

The doctor's eyes were on the journal, and there was a faint smile on his lips, but his voice carried a weight of seriousness.

Moé suddenly understood that this wasn't a joke. This was medical treatment. Matching the doctor's gravity, she replied, "I changed the cat's litter that day to a wood chip–based litter from the pet shop."

"I see. And how was that?" The doctor looked up.

"I thought it was a solid choice. The wood has a lovely scent, and it said on the package that the litter was low tracking. I thought it was good, but . . ."

"The cat didn't like it."

"Exactly."

The scent of hinoki cypress came back to her with an intensity, as if those wood chips were somewhere in the room. She recalled its pleasant smell and impressive deodorizing powers. But Kotetsu would not go anywhere near it. That night, Kotetsu had crouched into a Sphinx position, observing the plastic tray from afar.

He'll get used to it, she had thought.

But when morning came, the litter appeared as pristine as it did when she had first laid it out. It looked like Kotetsu had continued to avoid it. She didn't think much of it, left him food and water, and headed off to school.

She attended her lectures as usual and grabbed lunch with friends. When she got home in the evening and inspected the litter box, she was shocked.

The litter was still just as it had been when she had left it in the morning—no paw prints, not even the slightest sign of disturbance.

Moé started to panic. She had read somewhere online that cats are prone to urinary tract issues. The fact that the litter box hadn't been touched since the previous night was a worrying sign.

"It seems like he was doing his business . . . just not in the litter box," remarked the doctor as he continued to examine the Cat Record.

Moé nodded. "Mm-hmm, on top of some cardboard boxes."

She'd gone down on her hands and knees, crawling all over her bedroom, until she had found the bundled cardboard boxes, which she had intended to discard, now damp. Despite this evidence that the cat had finally urinated, and not in the designated place, she felt a profound sense of relief.

"After that, I went back to using the litter provided by this clinic."

"Hmm, it seems you've had quite a tough time." The doctor closed the notebook gently. "Some cats can't compromise when it comes to the smell of their litter. They won't go if they don't like the scent. Pleasant smells don't always equal good. Each cat has its own preference, which makes it all the more complicated. Litter might seem trivial, but in reality, it constitutes a not-insignificant importance in a cat's life. In other words, kitty litter is crucial to a cat," explained the doctor.

Moé listened vacantly, unsure what exactly she was being lectured on.

"Anyway, it seems like the cat was effective this past week." He peered into the pet carrier and gave it a pat on the top before taking hold of its handle. "Thank you for your efforts, Kotetsu."

"Ahh—" The sound tumbled out of Moé's mouth.

The doctor paused, resting his palm on the carrier.

Reflecting on this past week, Moé felt heat build behind her eyes. There was something unapproachable about Kotetsu's wild beauty, unlike her grandparents' cat, which she had been able to pet and scratch between the ears. For a cat with such a small head, his body was long, and when he lay on his side, he looked utterly content. She hadn't dared scratch his forehead, but she'd stroked his slender torso, lightly running her fingers from his neck to his butt and right to the tip of his tail.

"Bye-bye, Kotetsu."

Moé's eyes welled with tears. Kotetsu lay flat in the carrier facing her. It made her happy that he was looking at her.

"So now, it's time to say good-bye. Chitose! Please take the cat!" the doctor called out toward the white privacy curtains behind him.

The nurse pulled back the curtain and strode in.

Oh, Kotetsu's leaving me. Instinctively, Moé reached out, but then stopped herself.

In the nurse's arms was an identical pet carrier.

"Chitose, you're *so* on top of things. You've brought us another cat."

"This cat will also need to be managed," said the nurse curtly.

She swapped the carrier containing Kotetsu with the new carrier and disappeared behind the curtain.

The doctor turned the carrier toward Moé, revealing yet another cat inside.

"Shall we try this one now?"

Through the mesh door panel, the cat was giving

Moé a look. It had large eyes, and ears shaped like equilateral triangles. It was a lighter brown than Kotetsu but had the same distinct black stripes. Moé gave the doctor a glance.

"Is this one also a Bengal?"

"Indeed. They look similar but have different compositions."

Compositions? "Uhh . . . so am I going to carry on with the cat treatment?"

"Well, you haven't healed yet," the doctor said. "Take this cat home for a week. As before, please take notes on the diet and excretions in the notebook. I'll write you a prescription, so please collect the necessary items from the reception window before you leave."

The doctor pushed the pet carrier into Moé's arms— an unexpected second cat. As she walked past the reception window in a daze, the nurse called out to her. She handed her a paper bag about the same weight as last time, and inside was another instruction leaflet.

"*Name: Noelle. Female. Five months old. Bengal. Feed moderate amounts of cat food in the morning and at night. Water bowl must always be full. Clean kitty litter as needed. Will urinate two to four times a day; will defecate one to two times a day. Monitor the color, odor, shape, and volume of each excrement. To prevent urinary tract issues, it's important for both felines and humans to have stress-free elimination. That's all."*

As before, the leaflet only detailed things about the cat's bathroom habits.

"Um, excuse me."

"If you have any questions, please ask the doctor. Take care." The nurse turned her attention to some other administrative task.

Moé persisted. "This kitty litter is different from the previous one."

"Please direct your questions to the doctor. Take care."

"But kitty litter—"

"Take care."

"—is crucial to a cat."

"*Take care.*"

It's pointless speaking to this nurse. Let me ask the doctor. Moé began heading back into the examination room, when the nurse barked at her.

"Dr. Nikké is waiting for a patient with an appointment. If you have any questions, you can ask me."

She just told me to direct my questions to the doctor! Why is she acting like I'm doing something wrong? What a challenging personality. Moé felt herself growing angry, but because the nurse had remained so obstinate, she decided to swallow her irritation.

"I have a question about the kitty litter, the one you just gave me."

She took out the bag of litter and placed it on the reception counter. Unlike the litter that had been provided previously, this litter was paper based.

"I'm not sure if the cat will use this kind of litter. Kotetsu would only do his business in that gravel-like litter."

"Oh," said the nurse, as if thinking, *Is that her question?* "You can only figure out whether you like the litter by actually using it. The size, the feel under the paws. Stuff like that."

The nurse inspected her own palms, turning them upward and down.

"Like how it feels when you squeeze it between your fingers. I don't like the hard kind, but there are some who prefer it. If I remember correctly, Dr. Nikké is pro–hard litter. He said he likes the rustling feeling against his butt."

Moé tilted her head. *Is she talking about toilet paper?* A doctor named Nikké. A nurse named Chitose. She had no interest in either of their toilet paper texture preferences.

"Can you please give me the same cat litter as last time? It'll be a problem if this one doesn't use the litter box."

"In that case, please take the open bag of litter you just returned."

The nurse vanished from the reception window.

Moé began to wonder about the layout of the clinic. The building itself was tall and narrow, but the units didn't seem deep. The examination room seemed too cramped and unfurnished for conducting medical exams. She recalled the pet store she'd visited with Reona. There had been an unbelievable array of pet supplies packed tightly like books on a shelf. They likely stocked all that stuff because of customer demand, but she doubted such a variety was necessary for the animals. She suspected at least half of it was just for human satisfaction.

The nurse reappeared and handed Moé a bag with the remainder of the pebbly cat litter Kotetsu had used.

"Try out a bunch of cat litter. If you can't find a good fit, please come back." The nurse's tone was cool but not dismissive.

Now Moé had the kitty litter from before plus the new litter, and she also had the wood-chip litter at home. With three varieties, there was bound to be one that the new cat would like.

As soon as she got home, Moé clicked open the door to the carrier to release the cat, but this cat only stuck out her head. She had a round face, and there was a depth to her fur. She was indeed a lighter brown shade than Kotetsu, and her stripes bolder and more distinct. Despite their being the same breed, their features looked completely different. This cat's eyes were large and slightly slanted. She looked like a strong-willed girl.

"Nice to meet you, Noelle."

Moé stooped down to meet the cat's gaze.

Noelle flattened herself, then shot out like a bullet, running not under the bed but up the curtain.

It happened in the blink of an eye. Such velocity. Without any footholds, Noelle had climbed the wall. Perched skillfully on the narrow rod, she was now straining it.

"*Noelle!* That's dangerous. Come *down!*"

As she reached up, the cat lowered her triangular ears and bared her fangs. Moé hastily retracted her hands.

That's so scary.

Her grandparents' cat, with its large, pudgy face, occasionally grumbled with displeasure, but it never showed its teeth. This was the first time Moé felt truly threatened. If she reached out again, she was likely to be bitten or scratched.

Reluctantly, she gave up on bringing Noelle down and went to prepare her food and water. Into the litter tray, she poured the gravelly litter Kotetsu had used. After lining up all three, she decided to observe from a distance.

But no matter how long she waited, Noelle wouldn't come down. She'd dropped her stomach to the rail and inched back and forth repeatedly. She didn't seem to like it when her rump got close to the edge of the rail, as her hind legs would dangle down, making her shift forward again.

"Can't get down then, even though you're a cat?"

Shouldn't the cat scale the wall, just as she had on the way up? But apparently, she couldn't even do that, and just looked longingly at the floor. Whenever Moé reached up to her, she visibly recoiled.

"Then why did you climb up there? Oh, you have to be *kidding* me. What am I supposed to do?"

When she looked up the terms "cat" and "curtain rail" on her phone, all she could find were images of cats adorably sprawled on rails, with articles explaining cats' fondness for climbing them. But apparently, cats had a hard time descending butt first. To enable Noelle to jump headfirst, all Moé needed to do was create a platform at a nonintimidating height for Noelle to leap onto.

Not so easy, since she had no stepladder handy. *Something tall. Something a cat can use as a stepping-stone.*

"I got it! My suitcase!"

Pleased with her idea, Moé went to her closet, where her suitcase was tucked away at the very back. As she pulled out the items from the front of the closet, an avalanche of clothes and shoes cascaded down. She brushed aside the clutter and dragged out the suitcase. With this, Noelle could jump down safely.

"All right, Noelle!"

When Moé turned around triumphantly, she found Noelle by her feet, looking silently up at her. She then gracefully circled the room before she found her food and began to nibble on it.

I'm glad you're eating, thought Moé as she looked on. *But it would've been nice if you had come down a bit sooner.*

Her apartment looked as if she were in the middle of moving. Still, she was relieved to see the cat drinking water.

Noelle was more petite than Kotetsu. Her back was peppered with small, irregular rosettes, and black stripes marked her rear and legs. Save for the one patch on her back, she could easily pass for a tabby cat.

The pattern on her back, different from leopard print, was intriguing. *What could this pattern be? Big circles and little circles.* Her fur was somewhat long, so the pattern was a bit unclear, but there were four dots on each misshapen circle.

"Noelle, it looks like someone stepped on your back!"

The patterns on Noelle's back resembled animal paw prints, as if a cat had walked all over her. Moé let out a chuckle.

The cat looked over from her water bowl and tilted her head curiously.

Another week with a cat. It was unexpected, but it made Moé so happy, she couldn't stop smiling. Then the doorbell rang, and her smile vanished. *Shoot! It's Ryuji.*

Surveying her apartment, she took in the disorderly sight of all the stuff that had spilled out of the closet.

Clothes and shoes were strewn all the way down the hallway, too. There was no hiding it. She shut the door to her bedroom and stepped over the mess toward the front door.

Just as he had the previous week, Ryuji stood there, looking uncomfortable. She didn't want to let him in because of the disaster behind her, but before she could stop him, Ryuji was already peering over her shoulder. He looked appalled.

"Oh my god! What happened here? This place is a mess."

"Well . . . it was the cat."

"Wait, what? The *cat*?" He furrowed his brow and looked skeptically around his feet. "I don't see a cat anywhere. What happened? Is everything okay?"

"She's in my bedroom."

Seeing the worried look in his eyes, Moé opened the bedroom door. Noelle was nowhere to be found.

"Oh! Where did she go? Noelle? My little Noelle?"

She crouched under her bed and dragged off her comforter. *Where is she hiding?* When Moé finally stood up, she gasped. Noelle was atop the curtain rail again.

"*Noelle!* Why did you climb up again?"

The cat was sprawled along the narrow rail, her belly

and limbs balanced skillfully. Her stripy tail dangled and swayed gently.

Moé began to plead silently at the cat, *Please come down on your own again,* while Ryuji stood beside her, suspicion written all over his face.

"Hey, isn't that cat a different color from the other one?"

"Yes, it's a different cat."

Ryuji's skepticism was evident. Perhaps he was worried about the cat not being able to get down from the rail.

"I was given this cat at the clinic. They provided me with food and litter, and also a medication record— No, I mean a Cat Record journal."

"Okay . . ." Ryuji's eyes swept the room, scrutinizing every corner. "What's that?"

His eyes landed on the suitcase.

Shoot, I should have put that away.

"Oh, that? I took it out because I needed it for something, but I guess I should put it away."

"You have a cat to look after. I don't think it's time for you to be going away," said Ryuji.

"Uh . . ." Moé was taken aback by the unexpected remark.

He was refusing to meet her eyes.

"Look, Moé, I don't know the full story, but you shouldn't take in animals without thinking it through. Caring for them is a lot of work."

"This cat was prescribed to me at the clinic. Nakagyō Kokoro Clinic for the Soul in Nakagyō Ward."

"I see. I guess it's fine, then."

It's not fine at all. Moé tried to meet his eyes, but he wouldn't return her look. *Ryuji isn't worried about me. He just doesn't trust me.*

"I'm sorry. I think I better go home. We'll talk when things are calmer." He gave a small smile and left.

For a while, Moé stood completely still. She was shocked by Ryuji's words. It was indeed a strange story. A cat from a psychiatric clinic. A different one every week. But what he had said made it seem like Moé was randomly picking up cats only to neglect them. His judgment seemed a bit too harsh, no matter how reckless he thought she was.

She noticed Noelle was at her feet again, gazing up at her with golden eyes.

"Noelle, thanks to you, it looks like things are delayed again."

When Moé sank to the floor, Noelle lifted her nose

toward her. A cat had once again been effective at post-poning the breakup. But then, why did she feel so sad?

———

Reona listened quietly as Moé spoke, leaning back in her chair with a slight frown. It was Saturday, and the two were at a café on Karasuma Bukkōji Street. They saw each other a lot at school, but meeting over a popular dessert was a different story. The rich Basque cheesecake was worth the trip. Many of Kyoto's popular hangouts these days were either styled like speakeasies or nestled in traditional wooden town houses, and this café, too, had an old-world charm and was well reviewed.

"How can we get the cat to do her business comfort-ably? That's the question," said Reona, her face serious as she sank a slender fork into a moist and bouncy mat-cha Basque cheesecake.

"Yeah," agreed Moé. She had ordered a cherry blos-som cheesecake, and when she cut into it with her fork, it revealed a soft pink inside. "I definitely don't think she likes the current litter."

"Right. But since coming to your place, she's left 'product' in the litter box, right?"

"Of course."

As before, she'd been recording the cat's diet and litter box habits in the Cat Record journal. She had also started taking photos of them with her phone and showed several of them to Reona.

"What do you think? I don't think they look bad."

"Um, yeah. It all looks fine. You don't have to show me, though, thanks."

"She does her business regularly. But, every day, things are a bit different. Sometimes, she avoids the litter, or goes in the corner of the litter box, or she has accidents in the house. And I feel like after using the litter tray, she calls me over and looks at me like she wants to tell me something."

"Got it." Reona nodded gravely.

Four days had passed since Noelle had arrived. She was even more rambunctious than Kotetsu. Nothing escaped her interest. Moé's phone case was instantly destroyed, and then she pulled out all the stuffing from the cushions. The top of the curtain rail was her resting spot. She was also quick to climb onto Moé's lap, nuzzling the top of her head and flank against her; but any attempt to give her a pet sent her scurrying.

What really worried Moé was Noelle's behavior in the litter box. She didn't aggressively dig up the litter as

Kotetsu had done, but instead she sniffed and circled it. There was a noticeable restlessness about her. Moé was also bothered by the way she seemed to dart out of the litter tray after use.

Reona asked her about the litter situation.

"At first, I used the gravel-like one provided by the clinic, then I switched to the paper one. But I don't know—the litter seemed kind of . . . sad? . . . So yesterday, I laid down the hinoki cypress litter. She's been using all of them, but with great reluctance, I feel."

Moé had never imagined that the sight of a cat with whiskers drooping dejectedly could tug at her heartstrings so much. Noelle's eyes were always wide-open, her mouth tightly closed. Because she was so hard to read, her drooping whiskers seemed all the more sorrowful.

"So you've tried every kind of litter. In that case, maybe the problem isn't with the litter but something else. For example, the food."

"*Food?*"

"Yup." Reona scooped up the last bite of her matcha Basque cheesecake and looked up at Moé. "I've been about to say this since we got here, but I think we got unlucky with our table."

"Oh! You mean because of the bathroom?"

Moé had also noticed. The café had both counter and table seating, and they had been placed in a spot close to the bathroom. There was a lot of foot traffic from the customers who were using it, and there was even a line by the door. Whether they liked it or not, the bathroom was constantly catching their eye.

"Well, the café is crowded right now, so it can't be helped. But doesn't your appetite drop when the bathroom keeps appearing in your view while you're eating your cake? I'm sure even the people using it feel a bit self-conscious. Maybe there are cats, like humans, who don't like having their food and bathroom too close together."

"Now that you mention it, I've got her food, water, and litter box lined up next to one another in the same room."

"Why don't you try spacing them out a little? Or moving them to a spot where the smells don't mix."

"I'll give it a shot."

Moé felt like her perspective had suddenly broadened. *Yes, I can also be creative and try different things.*

She knew she had a tendency to slow down when she became too fixated on one thing. This reminded her of what the doctor had said. He had mentioned that she was a straightforward type of person but also that there were people who saw things only from their perspective and bent the truth to fit it.

She couldn't help thinking about what he'd said. She had intended to walk the straight path, but could she have veered off course without realizing it? Was it possible that because she wanted to move straight ahead, she had inadvertently bent the truth?

Reona had a part-time job in the evening, but there was still time until her shift, so they headed to Shijo Street to do some shopping.

"Hey, isn't that weird psychiatric clinic not too far from here?" asked Reona.

"Yeah, it's near Teramachi Street."

"It's funny that it prescribes you cats, but it's also a bit odd. My brother works at a cat rescue center, so I'm curious. Wanna check it out for a bit?"

Reona looked very eager. Moé didn't know how she felt about visiting the clinic for fun, but she figured it'd be okay to at least show her where it was. They headed north on Karasuma Street, passing Shijo Street and turning east onto Takoyakushi Street, leading them toward the clinic from the opposite direction that Moé had taken when she first visited it.

"So, is this clinic attached to a vet or a pet store?"

"I don't think so. It takes up a single unit in a tall, narrow building."

"Then I wonder where they get the cats. Maybe they're the doctor's cats? It sounds like a weird kind of clinic."

"Definitely." Moé laughed, but when she thought about it more seriously, it was indeed a bizarre story. No wonder Ryuji had been suspicious. Thinking about him made her heart sink, and her face clouded over.

"What's wrong? You look upset."

"I'm thinking about Ryuji. He said he's coming over again next Tuesday."

"You don't want to see him?"

"It's not that . . ." Moé averted her eyes.

If it meant they were going to break up, she didn't want to see him. Was that a contradiction? But she couldn't imagine whatever he wanted to talk about was good.

Reona kept her gaze straight ahead. "I don't like to comment about other people's boyfriends, but . . ." She fell silent and continued walking.

After a moment, Moé said, "It's fine, say what you're thinking."

"Really? Then I'll say it. I've always wondered how

he makes his girlfriend skip class every week just be-cause he can only meet on a Wednesday. What if you fail your classes? Is he going to take responsibility?" She paused. "Okay, that's it. I'm done with my comments," she said, her tone teasing.

The two walked in silence for a while.

Not too long ago, if anyone had criticized Ryuji, Moé would have said something back. But now, something was welling up inside her.

"You're right. He's not going to take responsibility."

"Exactly. That's why I'm so happy you've been com-ing to school lately. I mean, I sometimes prioritize my part-time job over class, so I can't really talk. Wait, we're already approaching Teramachi Street. Did we walk too far?"

"You're right. I don't think I went past Fuyacho Street."

Moé looked back the way they came. In Nakagyō Ward, the narrow streets crisscrossed like the grids of a Go board. There was no confusing Karasuma or Kawaramachi Streets, as they were major thoroughfares, but it was impossible to keep straight all the small side streets. Fuyacho Street ran south-north. Just one block west of it was Tominokoji Street. There were at most fifty meters between the two.

But there was no damp alley in view.

Moé stopped midway between the two streets.

"Maybe it's one more street over? This area is really confusing," said Reona.

"Maybe?" Moé couldn't quite remember it clearly herself. "That might be right."

"Let's go to the next street," said Reona, seemingly unbothered and heading northward to Rokkaku Street.

They circled the neighborhood, going up and down in all directions, but they couldn't find the alley.

"*Why?* Why isn't it here?"

"Wait! We should have looked it up on our phones from the start! What did you say this clinic was called?"

"Nakagyō Kokoro Clinic for the Soul. But it really should be around here. I've been to it twice."

"I told you, this neighborhood is confusing. I grew up in Kyoto, and I get lost around here. Okay." She peered at her phone. "Here you go. Wait, *what?*"

"What's wrong?"

"Nothing comes up." Reona's eyes were wide. "Not a single result. No website, no listings on medical sites, no reviews at all. How could it have zero online presence?"

My memory of it is fuzzy, and I have no information. Moé was starting to worry. But she knew she hadn't dreamed it. Noelle was at home, waiting for her to return.

"Oh, wait, there it is!"

Moé pounced on Reona's phone. "What did you find?"

"Dr. Kokoro's clinic. *Dr. Kokoro Suda of Suda Animal Hospital in Nakagyō Ward is a kind vet who is very knowledgeable about animals.* Oh, that's a vet? How misleading."

Hopes dashed, they continued walking and searching on their phones. No luck.

"Argh. I have to get to work. We'll have to give up this time."

Reona seemed nonchalant, but Moé began to panic. It might seem like she had made it all up.

"Reona, believe me, I was really prescribed a cat and then another cat. This clinic. It really exists."

Reona looked surprised by her friend's insistence. "Of course it does. If not, it'd be like a supernatural event, which is even scarier. More importantly, the cat's litter tray—comfort and cleanliness are key."

Relieved, Moé felt her eyes grow hot. Yes, when she got home, she was going to find a good spot for the litter tray where smells wouldn't get trapped so that Noelle could do her business more comfortably. She was going to make sure there was proper airflow. If the cat was feeling stressed, that was surely making her feel stressed, too.

— · —

It was Tuesday, the day Moé had to return the cat. This time, she didn't bring the leftover kitty litter. If she did have to give it back, she would buy more.

There was the alley, around the corner from the intersection where she and Reona had circled on Saturday. It wasn't so much an *I found it!* rush of excitement, but more of a contented *Ah, it was here* satisfaction that she felt.

When she opened the door, she saw the nurse sitting at the reception window. Her sharp features and stern demeanor accentuated her beauty. If Moé wasn't mistaken, the nurse's name was Chitose. She remembered because it, too, was beautiful.

"Ms. Ohtani, please head to the examination room."

Moé did as instructed and found the doctor waiting. She recalled that he, too, had an unusual name—Nikké.

Before Moé had even taken a seat, the doctor had begun to nod.

"Ahh, this is exactly what is supposed to happen, Ms. Ohtani. The effects of your cat prescription are kicking in, and you must be feeling drained. You have just one final push."

"Do you mean . . . ?"

"First of all, please show me the Cat Record."

The doctor pored over it as he had done the week before, while Moé clutched the pet carrier containing Noelle on her lap.

"Hmm. It seems this cat has gone through all available varieties of cat litter while ensuring you were aware of her disapproval. In other words, she's an *I shouldn't have to tell you* kind of girl. A bit of a high-maintenance type."

Is he actually analyzing the cat's personality? The carrier wobbled as Noelle began to meow.

"Oh, pardon me. I actually quite like girls like that, you know. I always try to anticipate what it is they want and act accordingly. If my guess is off-mark, I notice it immediately. I'm a *you don't have to tell me* kind of guy. I see, *I see*; when the litter tray was moved into the bathroom, she started using it with no trouble. The ventilation helped get rid of its odor. Thank you for going out of your way. Keeping an *I shouldn't have to tell you* girl happy can be a challenging task."

"Well, that's . . ."

It was true that Noelle gave off *I need to be pampered* vibes, but she was also a stubborn cat who rarely sought out affection. She was precisely an *I shouldn't have to tell you* girl. But Moé didn't mind. Being bossed around was part of caring for a cat, and it involved creativity and effort. And the cuteness that she got back more than made up for the trouble.

"Noelle has been a good girl. It's true that she wasn't easy to take care of, but she was truly wonderful."

"It seemed the cat was a good match. Now, shall we?" The doctor picked up the pet carrier. Moé felt the release of the weight from her lap.

"Chitose! Please take the cat!" the doctor called out toward the white curtain.

The nurse strode in, holding yet another pet carrier. She looked in a worse mood.

"Doctor, if you keep letting everyone skip the line, we might overlook the patient with an appointment."

He chuckled. "As a doctor, it's unacceptable to overlook a patient, but it's okay to make them wait a little. That's what we have the comfy chair for."

"Don't say I didn't warn you," said the nurse curtly. She switched out the pet carriers and disappeared behind the curtain.

"Don't pay her any mind. Our nurse can be a bit overbearing."

"I see." Moé felt a mix of emotions. She had gotten used to these strange exchanges, but the thought that she might have cut the line made her feel a bit guilty.

There was probably another cat in the new carrier in the doctor's arms. Was she going to be prescribed it for a third week? She felt simultaneously happy and sorry.

"Um, Dr. Nikké?"

"Yes, what is it?"

"Isn't it inconvenient if someone like me with such small problems keeps coming back? Nothing that warrants medical attention, anyway."

I don't want to be separated from the person I love.

Her heart sank as she recalled what had brought her here in the first place. Today was Tuesday. There was nothing to be excited about.

"There's no such thing as a big or a small problem,"

said the doctor, twisting his head as if bemused. "As with cat poop, size doesn't really matter. What goes in must come out. That's how it works. Naturally, if you eat a lot, a lot will come out. But even small poops, if they don't pass smoothly, can get stuck and build up, and before you know it, you're in a helpless jam. That's basically what constipation is."

Moé listened closely, but halfway through Dr. Nikké's explanation, her brow furrowed. *Since when did my problem become about constipation? Is that what it's really been from the start?*

"Well, if you take this new cat for a week, you will see huge improvements. Just a little while longer. You can do this!"

The doctor turned the pet carrier toward her. Through the mesh panel, she could see the equilateral triangular ears. She leaned in toward the carrier.

"Is this one . . . also a Bengal?"

"Yes, he is," said the doctor.

From what she could make out through the mesh, the fur was a completely different color from the previous Bengals. He was almost completely black. *I didn't know they came in this color, too*, she thought, staring unblinkingly.

"By the way, with this cat, what he'll take in is going to be more complicated than what comes out."

"What do you mean? I can't just give him the cat food you provide?"

"Apparently, he used to compete in cat shows and ate home-cooked meals of lamb and horsemeat to bulk up. He's retired now and has said good-bye to his swanky lifestyle. But I'm sure he'll eat anything when he's hungry. Now, take care."

The doctor pressed the carrier into her arms.

His attitude had been casual, but Moé felt like he had said something important. Managing what came out was already complicated, but apparently, what went in could be equally tricky. She wondered if she'd be able to get through the week.

The nurse was sitting at the reception window. After seeing this woman a few times, Moé now knew she wasn't being unfriendly for no reason. Her words might be harsh and her gaze pointed, but it was only because she was looking out for Dr. Nikké. Moé gave the nurse the prescription and was handed back a paper bag with a complete set of supplies—kitty litter, food, and an instruction leaflet.

"*Name: Bibi. Male. Six years old. Bengal. Feed mod-*

erate amounts of cat food in the morning and at night. *Water bowl must always be full. Clean kitty litter as needed. Will urinate two to four times a day; will defecate one to two times a day. Monitor the color, odor, shape, and volume of each excrement. To prevent urinary tract issues, it's important for both felines and humans to have stress-free elimination. That's all."*

It was just as she had expected.

She couldn't assume that the cat would accept the kitty litter right away. And there was a chance he would immediately reject the cat food.

From what she understood, it was her job to try different things with each of the cats she had been prescribed. *I'll do some research, get some advice, and devise a plan.* This time, the question she wanted to ask the nurse wasn't about the cat.

"Did I really cut in before a patient with an appointment?"

The nurse gave her a glance. "Don't worry. Everyone does it."

"If there's someone with an appointment next Tuesday, I'm happy to come by on a different day."

The nurse looked away. "I don't know if there *is* an appointment."

"Huh?"

"To begin with, I don't know if he's actually waiting for him," the nurse muttered. When she finally looked up, she had a faint smile on her face. "He's so loosey-goosey, I sometimes struggle to understand him. The doctor's patient is also peculiar like him. I can only wait patiently."

"I see."

So, does that mean I can cut the line?

The nurse, whose eyes seemed sorrowful today, was also a bit peculiar.

Just as Moé was about to leave, the nurse regained her blank expression and said, "Take care."

⸺ · ⸺

Bibi was larger than the previous two cats. His body was well toned, devoid of any flabbiness. His paws were as cute as squid ink dinner rolls, but his upper limbs were thick. He was svelte but had defined chest muscles.

His fur was like velvet. At first glance, it appeared completely black, but on closer inspection, it wasn't actually pure black but more of a bluish gray. No surprise— his ears were largish triangles, his face was small for his body, and he had a shapely snout.

If Bibi were human, he'd be a handsome Italian.

"Not that I've been to Italy," muttered Moé, who was watching Bibi gracefully roam around the room.

Bibi's movements were calm. He didn't dart under the bed or leap onto the curtain rail. But perhaps he was still waiting to see how things played out. She sensed his certainty radiating from his confident gait, that he was stronger and more beautiful than she would ever be.

It made total sense that he had competed in cat shows.

She watched as he drank a bit of the water. He seemed to avoid the cat food completely. Moé had set up two litter trays with the wood-chip litter—one near the bathroom and another in the corner of her bedroom. She had also bought an extra litter tray for cheap during Noelle's stay. Reona mentioned that it was a good idea to have multiple litter trays.

"Do you not like the food, Bibi? Preparing lamb and horsemeat is a bit too much for me."

Bibi wouldn't even sniff the food. Perhaps he wasn't hungry. *Even if your staple diet is Italian cuisine, when you're hungry, you'll eat white rice.* But just in case, she searched for cat food recipes online.

"Chicken and vegetables. Wow. They look simple, but you can't prepare them in bulk in advance."

While Moé was scrolling, Bibi seemed to have moved closer to her. *Maybe we'll bond more easily than I thought.* She decided to approach the cat.

But the closer she got, the more Bibi backed away. It seemed he hadn't let his guard down yet. But when she went back to browsing, Bibi again came near. He seemed curious.

"Come here, Bibi." Moé stretched out an open palm, but he retreated.

This cycle repeated endlessly. By now, they must have circled the room at least twice. Even now, Bibi was observing her from a distance.

Maybe it's against the rules for humans to approach first?

It was a one-sided rule, but whenever Moé stayed put, Bibi approached her. When she remained still, Bibi gradually came over and lay down sideways beside her. Moé was overjoyed just to have him come close to her.

She eyed his sleek, glossy black coat, which, upon a closer look, revealed a leopard-like pattern. It was sophisticated, as if from a refined Italian designer brand, and perhaps too understated for a flamboyant Osaka auntie. Bibi lay on his side for a while, then all of a sudden, he got up and moved toward his food bowl, sniffing around it for a moment. Slowly he took one, then two bites.

"I'm glad you're going to eat that, Bibi."

Just as relief was washing over her, Ryuji arrived. She had not forgotten this time. She took in his serious face as he stood at the door and realized she could no longer put things off.

Ryuji strolled into the apartment and froze. Bibi was in the center of her bedroom, grooming himself.

"Moé, this is wrong. It's just one cat after another . . . What happened to the others? Did you return them to the store where you got them?"

His eyes began to twitch. He had completely misunderstood the situation. Rather than anger, Moé felt disappointment.

"I've said this before, but these cats have been prescribed to me from a psychiatric clinic in Nakagyō Ward. It's a strange place. You'll see when you go there. I'm not making it up."

"I looked it up after you mentioned it last week. I couldn't find a single thing about this clinic."

"That's because . . ." Moé trailed off.

Ryuji pursed his lips.

What could she say to make him believe her? There

was nothing about the clinic online. She had no proof of its existence. Even if they headed there right now, they might not find it. But if they couldn't . . .

"Reona believed me."

Ryuji scowled. They both looked down, falling into a terrible silence.

"Moé?"

"Yes?"

"Is it normal for cats to leave food in their bowls?"

"*What?*"

She tried to meet his eyes. She had been sure he was just about to break up with her, but Ryuji was watching Bibi, who was giving his paw a good clean with his tongue.

"I have a dog at home, but he eats his meal in one go until nothing's left."

As Ryuji moved toward the cat, Bibi scampered away. He crouched by the food bowl.

"He's left most of the food. Is this normal?"

"Normal? Well, the others did the same. They ate their food bit by bit throughout the day."

Still, Bibi had eaten very little. In all likelihood, it was as the doctor had said—he was fussy about his food. But it annoyed her that Ryuji had pointed it out.

It was true that Moé could be unreliable. But she hadn't tried to avoid anything. For all three cats, she had researched the things she didn't know, thought carefully about their care, and even faced their smelly things head-on. She was no longer going to use her helplessness as an excuse. She had enough of trying to gauge what was going on in Ryuji's head.

"Bibi is used to high-protein, home-cooked meals. I don't think he likes commercial cat food. I'm going to cook for him as much as I can while he's here since he's a precious cat under my care. Rather than all this chat, why don't you just say what you have to say? You've been wanting to break up all this time, haven't you?"

"*What?*"

"I've been pretending not to notice, but I know you've been growing distant. You've come to end things, right?"

There was probably a better way for her to have expressed her feelings. But at the very least, she wasn't going to start crying. Moé blinked back her tears.

"What are you talking about? Why would I want us to break up?" asked Ryuji. He looked baffled.

Moé, too, was baffled.

"But—"

"It's true, I've been a bit distant lately—I'm sorry about that. It's just that I didn't know how to tell you . . . well, next month, I'm going to be transferred to the Tokyo office." Ryuji looked away awkwardly. "Once I'm in Tokyo, we won't get to see each other as often. Knowing how you dislike being alone, I couldn't bring myself to tell you. You don't handle things like this well."

A job transfer. To Tokyo. Moé was speechless.

From the side, she caught a glimpse of a black leopard-print cat. It was Bibi. He was sitting in the litter tray in the corner of her room, trembling.

He's going to the bathroom. So Bibi's okay with doing his business in the same space where he eats. I'll check on it later and note it down in the Cat Record.

What goes in must come out. It was that simple. Things became strained between people when they couldn't manage something as simple as that.

———

Moé showed Reona the picture she had taken on her phone.

"What do you think? Isn't it a bit small?"

"Well, yeah, I guess so. But I don't really pay that much attention to my cat's daily poops."

"I think the color and the texture are fine. But the amount is smaller than the previous cats'."

"But according to what's in this journal, it looks like the amount coming out matches the amount going in. Maybe it's just that this cat's a light eater?"

Reona was flipping through the Cat Record that Moé had brought.

Bibi was indeed a light eater. He left food in his bowl every day. Moé needed to be crafty. In addition to the cat food from the clinic, she tried giving him boiled chicken and vegetables, but he showed little interest. She couldn't leave the cooked food out, so while she was at school, she left cat food in his bowl.

"Well, even a cat eats less when he's not in his own home," Reona continued. "And it doesn't necessarily mean eating a lot is good. You're going to return him next Tuesday, right? If it's just until then, I think it's fine. He's eating and doing his business."

Moé took the Cat Record back from Reona. Lately, during their lunch break, it had become routine to have Reona check the photos of the cat's excretions.

Maybe she was being too open, or this was something borne from trust, or it was just Reona's personality. Whatever the case, Reona believed everything Moé said. This made it possible for Moé to talk to her about things she couldn't discuss with other friends. If that was what a mutual friendship was, she didn't have it with Ryuji.

Ryuji had not told her about his transfer because he found it difficult to bring up.

"I'm also worried about your boyfriend. If he moves to Tokyo, you won't be able to see him as often as you do now."

"I know. His day off is during the week, and it'll be hard to get to see him once a month, let alone every week. That's why he didn't want to bring it up. He said I get lonely easily and can't handle being alone."

"*What?* That's so rude. He's the one who can't handle being alone. He's been making his girlfriend take off school every week."

She could see that Reona was furious. But it had been Moé who had led her to believe the things she'd said about Ryuji. She was finally able to admit it wasn't fair.

"I'm sorry. That wasn't Ryuji. That was me."

"What was?"

"Ryuji actually told me that I shouldn't skip classes, but I wanted to be with him, so I did it anyway. It's no wonder he thinks I'm too dependent and unreliable. He couldn't tell me about his transfer because he was worried if he left me alone, I'd get sick from the stress. And look, just a little bit of tension in our relationship pulled me to that psychiatric clinic."

She had unnecessarily escalated a small misunderstanding. She should have confronted Ryuji directly the moment she thought he was behaving strangely. Avoiding unpleasant situations doesn't resolve anything.

"I see." Reona nodded. "So he's a decent boyfriend after all. I'm also sorry for assuming you'd fallen for him for his looks."

"No, that's on me for giving you the wrong impression. I was actually glad when you got mad just now. I really value how you always listen to my problems. Thank you."

"You're so straightforward. I have a hard time saying thank you to anyone," said Reona. "Well, maybe keep the cat poop photos between us. Most people won't appreciate them."

"I will."

"Also, speaking of stress, could it be that he's not eating much because he's not getting enough exercise? The cat, I mean. He's a Bengal, and I think they're an active breed."

"*Exercise!*"

It struck her then that, compared to the previous cats, Bibi was the least mischievous.

"Maybe it'd be good if you played with him more. Why don't you try teasing him a little?"

"But when I get close to him, he runs off."

"That's just how cats are. You have to get him off his high horse. Do you have toys? They love that classic teaser wand. Should we go buy one?"

"Let's go!"

Reona gave a hearty laugh.

How many times had they been to the pet store that month? The size of it no longer made Moé feel dizzy.

———

When Moé got home, Bibi emerged from her bedroom. Taking one slow step at a time, he cut a glamorous figure in black fur.

Because she'd made sure to store away anything a cat shouldn't mess with, he was able to roam freely. At six years old, he seemed pretty calm, and thankfully the curtains and sheets were still intact.

"Bibi, you're such a good boy."

When she reached out her hand, Bibi stopped. *Oh,*

that's right, I can't approach him. He has to come to me.
Well, in that case . . .

Moé took out the teaser wand she had just bought. Colorful strings hung from a long stick. The pet store was stocked with a ton of toys—motorized cushions, glowing balls, and even a figure-eight track toy that looked like something a human child would want. Everything looked so appealing, but she took Reona's advice that simple was best and opted for the basic, handheld teaser.

She crouched down and waved the toy. Bibi stared at her. Those eyes. He was definitely intrigued.

This will work.

She swung the wand left and right and slowly closed in on him.

Bibi's eyes were wide and trained on the toy. When it was almost in front of his nose, Bibi struck with incredible speed, snagging the end of the string. Once he took hold of it with his mouth, he wrenched the toy away and dashed off.

It had been swiped from her. In a matter of seconds.

Bibi sprawled on his side, chewing and scratching. He was definitely playing, but it wasn't exactly exercise.

She giggled to herself. "I thought this might happen."

From her bag, Moé took out another toy. Then another.

"What do you think? Double wands!"

She held two different teaser toys in each hand. Bibi let the string drop from his mouth. Apparently, even cats could be stunned.

"Here we go! Yeah, yeah, yeah, yeah, yeah!" She waved the two toys in the air.

Bibi hunched his shoulders, and then, in an instant, he pounced. Perhaps judging that he wouldn't be able to capture both toys at once, he leaped toward one toy, trying to snatch it away. Not to be beaten, Moé pushed and pulled on the toy, flicked it up high, and made it slither on the floor, engaging Bibi with lively movements.

"Wa, wa, wa, wa, wa, wa!"

Nonsense sounds kept flying out of her mouth as they both became lost in the moment. Bibi tugged on one of the cat toys, but Moé had anticipated the move. She let go and grabbed the cat toy Bibi had taken from her earlier. Bibi's pupils looked round in shock.

The cat's expressions. Surprise. Anger. Joy. It wasn't just in the movements; his whole body was radiating delight.

How long had they played?

Before she knew it, the cat toys were completely ragged. Only one toy was still intact, and Bibi had dragged it far away and was chomping on it tenaciously. Moé sank down. It was already evening.

"It's dinnertime . . . I have to boil some chicken."

All right. Here we go. She heaved herself up and went into the kitchen to cook some chicken tenders. When she turned around to look for the bowl of cat food, she was taken aback.

Bibi was nose deep in his bowl, ravenously gobbling up his food.

"W-wait a second, Bibi! Let me mix in some chicken for you!"

She quickly drained the chicken, let it cool slightly, and shredded it into fine pieces. She mixed it in with the cat food, and Bibi devoured it all with great gusto.

She was relieved. And happy. And completely worn-out.

She must have dozed off without realizing it and was woken by the sound of her door buzzer. When she looked at the intercom monitor, she saw that it was Ryuji. She ran to the door.

"What's up?"

"Moé, your hair is a mess."

"Oh, that, well— But this is the first time you're here on a Friday. Aren't you busy meeting clients on the weekends?"

"That's true, but I thought I should speak to you as soon as possible. I think we should—"

"Hold that thought!" Moé interrupted.

Bibi was just emerging from the litter tray in the corner of the room. Moé scurried over and checked inside. There was double the usual amount of poop, and it was carefully covered with litter.

"That's a big heap of poop. Good job, Bibi!" She was so happy that she turned to Ryuji and said, "Look, there's a big heap of good-looking poop."

"I-I see. A big heap. That's great."

They were both looking at the cat poop buried in the litter.

Even small problems can pile up when left unresolved. Feeling Ryuji's gaze on her, she turned to him. He was laughing.

"Let's give it our best shot."

"Yes, let's try our best." Moé nodded.

What goes in must come out. It might not be easy, but she was going to do her best.

On her lap, inside the carrier, was a cat.

As she sat in the examination room, waiting for the doctor, Moé reflected on the past three weeks. Each cat had been a handful. They had made a total mess of her apartment, leaving fur and cat litter everywhere. They had also given her a lot to worry about.

The white curtains parted, and the doctor came in. Before Moé could say anything, he raised the carrier up to his nose and began speaking to the cat.

"How was it? Did you have fun? Really? I'm *so* glad to hear it. Chitose! Please take the cat!"

The nurse strode in and swiftly took the carrier away. The doctor sat down before the befuddled Moé and gave her a warm smile.

"So, how are you feeling?"

There was a kindness written into his face. The loneliness she felt from seeing her cats leave was replaced by certainty.

"Even if I'm separated from the person I love, I'm going to keep trying my best."

"Is that so?" said the doctor. "That's great. Now, a

patient with an appointment is waiting, so we should wrap this up soon."

"But—" Moé blurted out. She didn't mean to cut into the other patient's time, but there was something she wanted to ask.

The doctor tilted his head. "What is it?"

"When I came to look for this place with my friend the other day, we just couldn't find it."

"Oh, I see. That's because Kyoto addresses are so confusing. 'North of this street' and 'east of that street.' The street names seem helpful, but they only make things trickier to figure out."

"But we circled this neighborhood over and over and couldn't locate the alley or the building. But today, I managed to find it straightaway."

"You'll find it when you're meant to," said the doctor matter-of-factly. Then he broke into a grin, like a child about to play a prank. "But don't go spreading the word about this clinic. We're not accepting any more new patients at the moment."

Suddenly, the curtains behind him swung open. The nurse glared at the doctor.

"Dr. Nikké, why are you subtly promoting this place? If you keep the rumor mill running, it's you who'll end up in trouble, especially with you always napping on the job!"

"I don't nap on the job." The doctor chuckled.

The nurse huffed and glared again before briskly pulling the curtain behind her.

Moé was dumbfounded.

"Our nurse really likes to fuss over things. Well, it's about time now. Take care."

"Um—"

"Yes? Is there something else?"

"This." Moé showed him the Cat Record journal. "What should I do with it?"

"Oh, you can keep it. When you feel stuck, go through it and remember the colors and shapes and such."

Colors and shapes.

"Oh, and smells. Now, take care!"

When Moé passed the reception window, she saw the nurse, looking unfriendly as always.

"Take care."

"Thank you!"

She closed the clinic door behind her and went out of the building. The ground, so damp beneath her feet, the sky, so vast as it stretched away into the distance—all of it was real. All of it existed.

She wondered if she would be able to come back if she ever had any more problems. The thought made it hard for her to walk away. But she knew she couldn't linger. There was probably someone else looking for it. Moé walked straight ahead and emerged onto the street, the name of which she didn't know. The street names in Kyoto seemed helpful, but they only made things trickier to figure out.

Ms. Michiko

2

—·—

Ms. Michiko

"So, you see, the neighborhood association's president's son-in-law's company's president's acquaintance went to the same place when his spouse passed away. It's not unusual at all. It's best to tell someone about these things sooner rather than later," said Ayumi, who had a loud voice and a frank personality, and was always full of energy.

Ever since her father-in-law, Tatsuya, had retired and handed over the household to his son, Ayumi had been managing the family's affairs.

"Be that as it may, I'm not sure these modern mental health clinics, or whatever you call them, are for me." Tatsuya Satonaka heaved a big sigh.

Until a few years ago, the Satonaka living room had

been a lively place. There had been his son and daughter-in-law, and his own wife, Meiko, too, with their grandson, Hayato, at the heart of the family. But Meiko had passed away six months ago, his son was always busy at work, while Ayumi had a part-time job. Even teenage Hayato was rarely around.

Tatsuya's daily routine was to laze about upstairs in the traditional Japanese-style room, come downstairs for meals, and then retreat back up. His only health issues were high blood pressure and high cholesterol. Other than some surgery for a hernia, undergone in his fifties, he'd been relatively healthy. It wasn't ill health that made him a recluse.

"But you haven't been out at all since your wife died," said Ayumi.

"Not true! I attended the neighborhood association meeting just the other day."

"That was four weeks ago. At the very least, you should go for walks. If you stay home all the time, your leg and back muscles will weaken. You don't need to worry, though. That acquaintance was healed at that whatchamacallit clinic in Nakagyō Ward. It's called . . . something therapy, where they listen to you talk for a little bit. Anyway, if you, too, become a shut-in, it's going to be a real problem. We already have one person who won't come out of his room."

Ayumi gestured toward the second floor with her eyes.

If that's the case, shouldn't Hayato, who barely leaves his room, go to that whatchamacallit clinic and get that something therapy?

But Tatsuya was helpless about how to handle his seventeen-year-old grandson. He was once an attentive, bright young boy. Before Tatsuya knew it, Hayato began to shut himself in his room. Even Ayumi, with all her positivity, was fretting about him.

"Try one visit. Just to pass the time."

Tatsuya paused for thought. "Where did you say it was?"

"Hold on, I had the neighborhood association president write it down for me." Ayumi took out a small slip of paper. "It's apparently *east of Takoyakushi Street, south of Tominokoji Street, west of Rokkaku Street, north of Fuyacho Street, Nakagyō Ward, Kyoto.*"

"What kind of address is that?"

"I'm not entirely sure, but it's somewhere around those streets. You can take the bus. You've got a reduced-fare senior transit pass. It'd be a waste not to use it."

It was true—two shut-ins in a single family were too

much. To put his son's and his daughter-in-law's minds at ease, Tatsuya reluctantly agreed to go to the Whatchamacallit Clinic in Nakagyō Ward.

— · —

Tatsuya was aghast. For a place with an incoherent address, he was able to find it quite quickly. But he didn't imagine it'd be on the fifth floor of a tall building with no elevator and only a steep staircase at the very back of the building.

He thought about turning around, but a few years ago, he'd been able to climb up five flights without a hitch. To give up here was to admit his decline.

He glanced up the stairwell to see what looked like a half-landing between each floor. *I got this!* He began his ascent with enthusiasm, but when he reached the landing before the third floor, he found he could no longer lift his legs. He was surprised by how incredibly weak they felt.

This is not good.

His knees were stuck—he could not muster any strength. The only thing he could do was wait to get his breath back, then make his way down the stairs. Tatsuya hung his head, disappointed in himself.

"Hey, Gramps! What's up?"

Tatsuya jumped. Someone was coming up the stairs—a shady-looking man with a deep tan in a bold shirt and an equally bold expression. In no time, the man was standing on Tatsuya's landing. "Gramps, what floor are you headed to?"

"Well, I had something to do on the fifth floor . . ."

"The fifth floor?" The man's eyes sparkled. "Then you're a customer of mine. I'm the only person with an office on that floor. I'm Akira Shiina, protector of Japan's health."

"What's that?"

Could this man, dressed like this, seriously be affiliated with the clinic? His peculiar self-introduction only made him seem more suspicious.

"Come on, Gramps. I'll give you a piggyback ride."

"Oh, no, no, no, that's okay."

"Don't be shy. Thanks to this magnetic necklace, I might be nearing thirty-seven, but my body's only in its twenties," said the man called Shiina as he pulled out the thick, silver necklace hanging around his deeply exposed chest.

Not good. This man is totally sketchy. I didn't realize the "something" therapy was this kind of thing.

But Shiina had turned his back toward him and was crouching down. The heat radiating from his large body was immense, and on this narrow landing, there was nowhere to run.

Tatsuya reluctantly allowed the man to carry him, and without the slightest wobble, they began to climb the stairs.

"So, how old are you, Gramps?"

"I-I'm seventy-eight."

"If that's the case, you've got to give this a go. Living long is no good if you're not healthy. There've been a lot of longevity businesses cropping up lately, but most of them are bunk. But our magnetic necklaces are the real deal. If you wear this, you can climb up stairs with no effort. There's even a three-year warranty. Since you made it here, if you buy our best one, we'll cover the installment-payment fees."

Chatting nonstop, he carried Tatsuya all the way to the fifth floor. The fifth-floor hallway was lined with old metal doors and was as dimly lit as the rest. Shiina, still in high spirits, headed straight to the door at the very end. A plate on it read JAPAN HEALTH AND SAFETY ASSOCIATION. This was clearly not where Tatsuya had imagined he would end up.

"I don't think this is the right clinic," said Tatsuya.

The smile vanished from Shiina's face. "Again with the 'clinic.' Why do you keep mentioning it, Gramps? Where did you hear about it?"

"Where? From the neighborhood association's . . . acquaintance of an acquaintance of an acquaintance."

"A mental health care kind of place?"

"Exactly."

"My business is the only one on this floor. I don't know why, but people keep mistaking the unit next to mine for that place. But that unit's vacant. People go in and come out immediately."

"I *see*."

Tatsuya frowned. *Do I have the wrong information? Or did the clinic close?*

Seeing Tatsuya's disbelieving face, Shiina rattled the doorknob of the next-door unit.

"See, it's locked. That place has quite a bad history."

Tatsuya placed his hand around the doorknob and twisted it.

Shiina's face changed color. "*Huh?* It actually turned. Did they forget to lock it?"

Shiina pulled hard on the doorknob, but something wasn't right.

"Wow! This door's really heavy."

He grabbed the doorknob with both hands and braced his legs. His body shook with effort, but the door wouldn't budge.

"You have got to be kidding me. I am the protector of Japan's health. There's no way I can't open this door. *Aargh!*"

Shiina's roar echoed through the deserted hallway. Finally, the door began to give. Shiina sat down cross-legged on the floor to stop the door from closing.

"Look at this, Gramps. This is the power of our magnetic necklace."

He was panting, but his smile was brimming with confidence.

Tatsuya craned his neck and peeked inside. The room was a bit dark but appeared neatly, though sparsely, furnished. There was no one behind the small window at what appeared to be reception.

"So, it *is* a clinic."

"Huh?"

Shiina remained seated on the floor and leaned over to take a look inside. His mouth fell open.

This guy is so over-the-top, thought Tatsuya. He thanked him for getting the door open and for giving him a piggyback ride, then stepped inside. He thought Shiina might follow him, but Shiina, hunched over with fear and mouth still agape, pushed the door shut. It seemed like Tatsuya had gotten away with not having to purchase that questionable necklace.

There was a loud *clank* from behind him, followed by the sound of slippers pattering on the floor. A young, pale nurse appeared.

"Can I help you?"

"Is this a mental health . . . something clinic?"

"Mental health something?" The nurse gave a slight frown. "This is Nakagyō Kokoro Clinic for the Soul, not a 'mental health something' clinic."

It seemed the nurse didn't appreciate the sloppy phrasing, but at least it was clear this was the place he had been looking for. Tatsuya smiled wryly.

"I'm sorry about that. I wasn't given the full name. I know I don't have an appointment, but is there any chance I could see someone now?"

"I see. You're a patient. Please go ahead into the examination room."

Tatsuya was relieved. He had gone out of his way to come here. As long as he was seen by someone, it should appease Ayumi. As he walked into the examination room, the privacy curtains in the back parted, and the doctor, a mild-looking young man in a white lab coat, appeared.

"Hello! It's your first time at our clinic, isn't it? How did you hear about us?"

"How?" Shiina had asked him the same question just now, but Tatsuya didn't remember exactly. "Through an acquaintance of an acquaintance. It was my daughter-in-law who said I should come."

"I *see*. We're not taking on new patients at the moment, but I'll make an exception for you as you're a referral. What's your name and age?"

"Tatsuya Satonaka. I'm seventy-eight."

"What brings you in today?"

"Well . . . six months ago, my wife passed away suddenly. Since then, life has felt tedious and irritating. I'm personally okay with feeling this way, but my son and his wife are worried that I might become a recluse."

"A recluse, I see."

"My grandson's in a similar state. He's only seventeen, but he's turned basically nocturnal. He stays holed up in his room during the day and then is up all night on his computer or something. I don't even know if he's attending school. I know it's not my place to say, but I'm worried about his future."

Having put it into words, Tatsuya realized his family was dealing with serious problems. But when he looked into the doctor's face, he was taken aback. The doctor was laughing.

"There's nothing wrong with being nocturnal. The night is more fun anyway."

"More fun?"

"Yes. And it's quieter and better for hunting. And you can see more clearly in the dark."

Tatsuya cocked his head. *I don't understand.* Had he missed something, or was that really the doctor's opinion?

On the opposite side of this narrow room, the doctor sat at his computer and began typing on his keyboard.

"Anyway, just in case, let's warm you up a bit. Chitose! Please bring in the cat!" the doctor called out toward the curtains.

The same nurse who had been at reception walked in. When Tatsuya saw what she was holding in her arms, he felt his heart start to race in astonishment.

Is that an actual cat?

It was indeed an enormous black-and-white cat. Most

of it was spilling out of the nurse's arms. Its limbs stuck out straight, its face was buried in its body, and perhaps because it was plump, it looked especially uncomfortable.

"Dr. Nikké, quickly! She's heavy! I'm going to drop her!"

The doctor took the cat from the nurse, placing its chin on his shoulder as if he were carrying a child.

"Wow, she is heavy. How much does she weigh?"

"I have no idea. You need to come pick up the hefty cats yourself."

The cat must have been quite heavy, because the nurse's pale cheeks were flushed and her eyes were narrowed angrily.

"Good grief, spoiling the cat like this has made her so chonky. One of these days, her collar's going to snap."

The nurse left in a huff, as the doctor gave the cat's butt a pat.

Tatsuya fell into his seat. He had never seen a cat this large in his life. He could see only the cat's back as she sat splayed in the doctor's arms, but at any rate, it was a wide expanse of white with black patches. Her fur was long and reminded Tatsuya of a carpet.

How much does that cat actually weigh?

As if reading his thoughts, the doctor said, "She's

part Maine coon, a breed of big cats. She was a large kitty to begin with, but her caretakers pampered her so much that she's grown even bigger. But she'll be more effective at this size. Now, where shall we warm you up?"

The doctor shook himself and adjusted his hold on the cat. Even though he was a young man, probably around thirty, he seemed to be struggling to hold the cat's weight. As Tatsuya was speculating that the cat probably weighed at least ten kilograms, the doctor crossed the examination room, brushing along the wall, to stand behind him.

"Shall I place her on your shoulder?"

"What?"

Before he could think, *Surely not!*, the cat had been draped facedown over his shoulders, and in an instant, her face was buried in Tatsuya's thigh.

"Ouch, ouch, ouch!"

"Oh! Was that the wrong spot?"

The pressure on his shoulders lifted suddenly.

Tatsuya was so shocked he couldn't even blink. A cat so gigantic that he thought his back might snap had been plopped over his shoulders. Now, she was back in the doctor's arms, dangling limply like a burlap sack.

"The spot that hurts isn't always actually the problem

area. It's sore because a different spot is pulling on it and creating tension. So, it's better to apply the cat on the other spot instead of focusing on where you feel the pain."

"Apply the cat?"

What in the world was this doctor talking about? As Tatsuya was pondering what he should do, the doctor walked in front of Tatsuya and lowered the cat onto his lap.

"Okay, please hold on tight."

"Uh, w—"

Before he could refuse, the doctor had let go. Tatsuya quickly caught the cat in his arms. It dropped its butt onto his knees and squished comfortably into a pile.

"Wow, this is impossible," he said. *I'm going to drop the cat. It's going to slide off!*

Back when his family had still been a happy unit, they had attended the neighborhood association's mochi-pounding event together. The mochi made with a traditional mallet and mortar was gooier than machine-pounded mochi, and it had almost slipped out of his hands. He remembered how everyone had laughed uproariously as he struggled not to drop it.

It feels exactly the same.

This cat is like mochi. Freshly pounded mochi.
Remember the sensation of that mochi.

The cat's butt was about to slide off. Tatsuya gathered the cat in his arms, carefully rotated her pudgy belly and spine, and finally managed to position her four legs underneath. He grabbed the cat's rump firmly with both hands and placed her cheek against his chest. While all of this was taking place, the cat remained glumly compliant.

How is she so floppy? Won't a cat feel uncomfortable if her jiggly tummy's about to tumble off? As Tatsuya wondered, *What kind of animal is this?,* he let out a deep sigh.

The doctor sat before him. "How is it? Do you feel a tingling sensation?"

Tingling sensation? It reminded Tatsuya of the low-frequency muscle stimulator pads they placed on his back at the chiropractor's. He shook his head.

"I see. But do you feel a slight warmth?"

"Well . . ."

Now that the doctor had mentioned it, he could feel the cat's warmth through his clothes. The cat not only had a large area but also had a very long coat. Her ears were sharp triangles, with long hairs growing on the inside as well as the outside. The tips of her ears were tufted like the bristles of a calligraphy brush. He had thought cat ears were simply thin, triangular flaps of skin, but experiencing them up close like this, he realized they were fuzzy with ear hairs like his own.

No, they were different from his ear hairs. His own ear hairs were not this fine and soft. *A warm creature with cute ear hairs.*

Tatsuya nodded earnestly.

"Then let's leave her there for a bit. Oh, so what was it you were telling me? Six months ago, your wife passed away, and now everything bothers you. So you've started binge eating and drinking, constantly filing claims with customer service, trolling people on social media, ding dong ditching, littering empty cans—"

"Wait a second!" Tatsuya was dumbstruck. "I'm not sure what you're talking about, but none of that's true."

"Oh, is that so? So, your wife passed six months ago . . ."

"That part is correct. She died suddenly from a stroke. Just collapsed out of the blue. It all happened so quickly. It still doesn't feel real to me."

"But you must feel it, right, since everything started feeling tedious and irritating for you?"

"So, you *were* listening to me."

The doctor chuckled. "If someone who used to be around is not anymore and it has changed you, there's a reason for it. People say it's a bad thing to be a recluse, but I don't think there's anything wrong with it. You're choosing to withdraw from society because you want to."

"Well, it's not that I want to withdraw from society. Well, in my case, maybe I do like to laze about at home, but there are plenty of people in the world who want to go outside but just can't."

"You mean like, they're locked up?"

"Huh?"

"Like there's a lock on their cage?"

The doctor had a faint smile on his face, but it was impossible to read what emotions lay within.

Tatsuya felt a chill go down his spine. The cat lifted her chin and gave him a look.

Buried in the cat's thick fur and folded into her flesh was a pink, worn-out collar. Just as the nurse had said, it seemed too tight for her chubby neck.

Isn't it dangerous for a collar to be that tight? thought Tatsuya.

"I don't know much about cats, but is it okay for her collar to be this snug?"

"Hmm? Let me see." The doctor leaned forward so

close that he was almost in Tatsuya's arms. "Oh, you're right. It's almost at its limit. Okay, let's take it off, then."

The doctor buried his hands around the cat's neck, removed the pin from its notch, and undid the buckle, revealing an indentation in the fur around the cat's neck. The doctor seemed very accustomed to handling animals, almost as if he was a vet. Tatsuya wondered if the cat had been uncomfortable, but after giving herself a good shake, all sign of the collar disappeared. And once again, she looked grumpy.

"This cat's very tame. She seems not to mind anything," said Tatsuya.

"She's too lazy to even care. This is what true laziness looks like."

"I see."

The argument was oddly compelling. Even Tatsuya was more active compared to this cat. He would have at least readjusted his position himself before allowing a stranger to scoop him up by his butt.

He became aware of a numb feeling creeping up his legs. This enormous cat definitely weighed over ten kilograms.

"My legs are starting to tire."

"Feeling any tingling?"

"Tingling . . . I think it's just that my legs are all pins and needles because of the weight of the cat."

The doctor gave a laugh. "So your grandson—what's going on with him again? If he's become nocturnal, it's better if he has a reflective layer of tissue in his eyes, one that bounces light back to his retinas, so he can see in the dusk. It allows in a lot of light and enhances your vision. You should ask your grandson about it. It's pretty neat."

Tatsuya couldn't tell how serious the doctor was. Was it all a joke, or was he recommending some kind of therapy?

"My grandson wears contact lenses, so I don't think that'll work for him."

"That's too bad. It's really handy, you know. People say being nocturnal is a bad thing, but that's not true. By not seeing what you don't need to see, you only focus on what you absolutely need to. Kind of like how a cat can walk the streets at night with just a little bit of light."

"A little bit of light . . ."

"Is at least a little bit of light reaching your grandson? Or not at all? Is he in complete darkness?"

Tatsuya didn't know how to answer the doctor's insistent questions.

Was it pitch-black in Hayato's room? If so, what

could he do as a grandfather to help him? Did Hayato have enough strength to navigate with minimal light like a cat? When he dropped his chin toward the cat, he saw its mysterious eyes. Although they had a solid shape, they somehow appeared half liquid.

"Cats' eyes are like water manjus."

"Water manjus?" The doctor burst out laughing. "That's a new one. Those jiggly, jellylike confections, right? Are they tasty?"

"Yes, they're like transparent dumplings with smooth bean paste in the center. I . . . like them."

Tatsuya glanced down. He was losing all sensation in his legs. The numbness was becoming too much to bear.

"Can you please move the cat? I think I've had enough."

"It seems so. Did it loosen you up?"

Quite the opposite. My legs feel like logs. But if I say the wrong thing, who knows what this doctor will do to me. Tatsuya nodded until the doctor hauled the cat off him. The moment the pressing warmth had lifted, blood rushed into his legs. Tatsuya gritted his teeth.

"Job well done," the doctor said into the cat's ear. Then, "Chitose! Can you please take the cat?"

The curtains parted with a *swish*, and the nurse

strode in. She staggered a bit as she carried the cat in her arms toward the back.

For a while, Tatsuya couldn't move. Once the numbness had eased a bit, he looked up to see the doctor slumped on his desk with his mouth open. He seemed to have suddenly fallen into a nap.

"Um, doctor?"

The doctor didn't wake. There was a faint whistling sound as he breathed. Perhaps his nose was stuffy.

It was the first time Tatsuya had encountered a doctor, a clinic, or a treatment like this.

He stood up slowly and, with stiff knees, shuffled one step at a time out of the examination room. He staggered past the reception, but there was no one in sight.

This clinic is too strange. I'm never coming back here.

As he was about to waddle out of the clinic, the nurse appeared in the reception window.

"You left this behind," she said, presenting him with the pink collar. The leather was cracked, and the holes were stretched. Tatsuya blinked.

"No, that's not mine."

"You left this behind."

"That belongs to—"

"You left this behind."

"—to the cat just—"

"You left this behind!"

The nurse spoke over him. She held the collar out to him, glaring with an intense, imposing stare.

What is with this clinic?

Tatsuya accepted the collar with a shudder and stowed it quickly in his pocket. If he dawdled, they might apply another cat on him. He pushed open the door and emerged into the hallway. Just as the door was about to close, a voice rang out. "Take care!"

—⋅—

"Ouch, ouch, ouch!"

This is the second time.

Tatsuya sprang up from his futon, clutching his left toe with both hands.

"*Another* cramp! Ouch!"

First, it had been the right foot; now, it was the left. Waking up to the sudden charley horses was panic in-ducing. He clenched his teeth and rubbed his calf. He was certain it was holding that cat for so long at that clinic that was to blame. Now, here he was at night, his muscles howling with agony from his bad circulation.

The pain began to subside, but there was still a fuzzy sensation in his leg.

"This is not good."

Tatsuya changed into some clothes lying nearby and left his darkened room. He was worried that if he didn't move around, both his legs might cramp next. Light and the sound of the television leaked from the living room. It was only nine o'clock, but still, a bit late for an old man to go on a walk. Not wanting to worry his son and his daughter-in-law unnecessarily, he slipped quietly out of the house.

The sky was pitch-black; a few streetlamps illuminated the street.

It was a residential neighborhood, so there were no stoplights, and even during the day, there was little traffic. When Meiko had been around, they had taken walks arm in arm in the early evening, and he seemed to recall that once the sun started to set, it became hard to see in the fading light. Surprisingly, once the sky became completely dark, it was almost brighter out, and there was no need to strain one's eyes to see.

How many years had it been since he'd walked around at night? He was familiar with all the streets in the neighborhood, so he wasn't worried. Sooner or later, his legs should loosen up. Instead of going to some weird clinic, a nighttime walk like this was just what he needed. It was a suitable amount of exercise and a nice change of scenery.

Tatsuya stopped walking. He had wandered toward one of the wider streets in the neighborhood. An empty road stretched out before him.

Oh, that's right.

This was the street he and Meiko used to amble down together. They didn't really talk about anything in particular on these walks or even enjoy the scenery. It was just part of their daily routine to stay healthy.

Still, it was the same scenery they'd seen every day. He didn't like recognizing that his wife was no longer in it. He also didn't want people looking at him pityingly when they saw that the two-person walk had become a solo one.

It was really beginning to sink in. His wife was gone.

He hovered in the same spot for a while. When he finally decided to head back, he noticed a bulletin board. It was the kind of public board set up in every neighborhood by the local government, and it was plastered with a variety of notices and public service announcements. It was under a streetlamp, so he could read the contents clearly, even in the dim light. One particular notice caught his eye.

"Grandpa?" someone suddenly called out.

To Tatsuya's surprise, it was his grandson, Hayato, on his bike.

"What are you doing, Grandpa?"

Hayato hopped off his bike and sauntered over. He had earbuds in, a phone in one hand, and a large backpack slung over his shoulder. It looked like he was getting back from somewhere.

"What about you? What are *you* up to?"

"Just getting back from school. Isn't it unsafe for you to be wandering around at this late hour?" said Hayato with a curious look, his tone somewhat childlike. Though they saw each other every day, it had been a while since they'd had a proper conversation.

"School? You go to school?"

"Yeah, I do. At night, though."

"Since when?"

"For a while now." Hayato looked bemused. He turned his gaze to the notice board.

"What's this? What were you looking at?"

"This? It's a bulletin board. Do you know when this flyer went up?"

"No idea. I didn't even know there was a bulletin board here."

Hayato leaned in closer to the board.

"Oh, it's about a cat. What about it?"

"Yeah." Tatsuya stood at Hayato's shoulder and gazed at the board.

It was a flyer about a missing cat. It had handwritten details with a picture of a cat stuck on with glue, and even in Tatsuya's opinion, it was crudely made. It included the owners' names and phone number.

"Do you know the people looking for the cat, Grandpa?"

"I recognize their names and faces. They're the Watanabe couple from the next neighborhood over. They might be a bit younger than me."

"I see. If they're trying to find their cat, it's better if they post this on social media. Maybe they don't know how. No one's going to look at this flyer on this bulletin board."

"But we looked at it."

"Huh?"

"I know this cat."

There was no doubt it was the gigantic cat from Nakagyō Kokoro Clinic for the Soul in the picture. The grumpy expression. The long white coat with black patches. She was sitting on her belly on a tatami mat with her hind legs splayed out. On the flyer, it read NAME: MS. MICHIKO and also that she had been wearing a pink collar when she disappeared.

"It says 'Ms. Michiko,' but do you think they wrote 'Ms.' on purpose? Do you think they actually call her that?"

"Of course."

"How classy. That's pretty cool, actually. So where did you see this cat, Grandpa?"

"At the clinic."

"That's good that they found her. You should let the owners know."

"I should let them know where the clinic—"

Tatsuya had a thought. *Would that peculiar doctor and nurse handle things properly? What if they refused to return the cat, claiming she was a hot pack or a low-frequency muscle stimulator device?*

"No, I'm going to go to the clinic tomorrow to check."

Hayato frowned. "Shouldn't the owners go?"

"If it isn't their cat, they'll be really disappointed."

"But can you tell whether it's the lost cat or not? I feel like the owners would be able to tell for sure."

"No, it'll be fine," insisted Tatsuya.

Hayato wasn't convinced. In the end, they decided to go to the clinic together.

———

The next morning, as the two of them were getting ready to head out, Ayumi, eyes wide, exclaimed, "You're going out this early, Hayato? And with your grandfather?"

"Yup," Hayato answered as he slipped into his shoes.

Ayumi's expression made it clear that it was incredibly unusual for Hayato to be going out during the day. Instead of being worried, she seemed a bit emotional as she saw them off.

The clinic in question was in the same ward as their home, just a short bus ride away. It felt refreshing for Tatsuya to go out with just his grandson, even if it made him a little nervous. When they boarded the bus, Tatsuya attempted to lead Hayato to an open seat.

"I should be the one doing that, Grandpa," said Hayato with a smile, just as adorable as in his younger days. His smile had not changed at all. As Tatsuya swayed in his bus seat, he realized he no longer needed to look after his grandson on outings anymore. Unknowingly, Hayato had crossed the threshold of adolescence and was on the verge of adulthood.

When did he start going to night school?

How long is he going to live this nocturnal life?

Did he really choose a path different from the norm?

As he absent-mindedly pondered these things while looking out the window, Tatsuya recalled something the doctor had said. *A cat can walk the streets at night with just a little bit of light.*

"Hayato?"

"Hmm?" Hayato was on his phone, standing at his grandfather's shoulder.

"I took a walk last night, and I realized I can walk quite a bit."

"Yeah?"

"Being nocturnal might not be too bad, you know. When it's dark, you can avoid seeing unnecessary things."

"Really?"

"Yes. And night school's not a bad idea. That's all part of life."

"True."

Hayato was absorbed in his phone. While Tatsuya

and Ayumi were worried about the challenges Hayato might face in the future, to him, this was just life as he knew it. Cats—whether they were day cats or night cats—picked their own hours to be active.

They got off the bus on Oike Street. The buses didn't go down the narrow, grid-like roads.

"Grandpa, what's the name of the street where the clinic is?"

"We take Fuyacho or Tominokoji Street and turn on Rokkaku or Takoyakushi Street."

It was roughly three hundred meters from the bus stop—about a five-minute walk. Or at least that's what he remembered.

"Huh? Did we go down the wrong street?"

Tatsuya was leading the way, but he couldn't find the alley from yesterday on any of the four streets. After circling the area twice, they found the building on Fuyacho Street. From the outside, it looked identical to the building he'd seen yesterday. But something was different. The building with the clinic had been situated farther back from the street. Hayato looked perplexed as he watched Tatsuya gazing up at the building.

"What's wrong, Grandpa? Is this not it?"

"No, this is the building. But also not the building."

It was a narrow, five-story structure with an old nameplate that read NAKAGYŌ BUILDING. He fearfully peeked into the open entrance and spotted a staircase at the end of the hallway. *It is definitely the same place.*

"Oh look! It's Gramps from yesterday!"

Tatsuya jumped. He turned to see a man approaching him with a grin. With a loud shirt and a deeply tanned face, it was none other than the sketchy president of the company that made the magnetic necklaces.

"The protector of Japan's health . . ."

"That's right. Akira Shiina, president, at your service. I knew you'd come back for our necklaces. Oh, and you brought family with you today. All good, all good. I know the necklaces aren't cheap. There'll be fewer disagreements later if you get your family's approval first."

The volume of his voice and his intense vibe were as overwhelming as yesterday. If this man existed, it meant that it hadn't been a dream. That doctor and nurse and the giant cat, Ms. Michiko, were all here.

Tatsuya sauntered into the building. The somewhat puzzled Hayato followed after him. The row of metal doors in the dim light all looked the same. Hovering at the bottom of the staircase, Tatsuya gathered his energy.

But just as he was about to begin climbing, Shiina stopped him.

"All right, Gramps! Leave it to me again today."

"What? No, no, I—"

"Don't be shy. I am an ally of the aging population. It's only natural for a youngster to carry an old person on their back. Right, kid?"

Hayato maintained a stoic expression. Trapped in a narrow hallway where there was no room for more debate, Tatsuya reluctantly allowed Shiina to carry him up to the fifth floor. Impressively, Shiina didn't seem winded at all. On the other hand, Hayato, who followed them up, was gasping for air.

"Hah! Kid, you might need the magnetic necklace, too. Our necklaces are luxury items, so minors need approval from their parents, but don't worry. I have an older model that's cheaper."

"Oh, all right," said Hayato. "Grandpa, is it on the fifth floor?"

"Yes. Second unit from the back."

"*What?* The clinic again?" Shiina recoiled dramatically. "Wait a second. Gramps, aren't you here to buy my necklace?"

"No, I actually came here today to see the cat."

Tatsuya looked in the direction of the second unit from the back.

Shiina's face clouded.

"Did you say 'cat'?" His voice sounded different. His eyes began to turn dark. He was almost a different person.

"There are no clinics or cats in this building. That unit is empty."

"But you opened the door for me yesterday."

"That was some sort of misunderstanding. Don't drag me into any weird situations."

Shiina stood in front of the door to the clinic, breathing audibly. Then he grabbed hold of the doorknob and started to twist it right and left. Tatsuya gave him a look. Hayato tilted his head in confusion.

"Hey! Anyone in?"

The door seemed locked. Shiina broke into a wide grin, rattling the knob like a child.

"See, look! No one's in."

"Maybe they're closed today?" said Hayato in a small voice.

"Nope. There hasn't been a tenant in this unit in years. It's a stigmatized property with a shady history."

Shiina stepped back from the door and sighed solemnly.

"I'm only telling you because you brought it up, but some time ago, they used to grow cats in this unit. They were illegal breeders, but due to sloppy management, they went bankrupt, and the owner skipped out, leaving all the cats behind."

Hayato, who had been feigning disinterest, now looked disgusted. "Does that mean that the cats were trapped in here?"

"*Exactly*. From what I heard, the owner left behind a ton of them. The employees apparently tried to find the cats homes, but there were so many. In the end, a bunch were left in their cages, and no one came for them. You can imagine what happened. I don't have a cat, but just thinking about it makes my chest tighten. Even the owner of the building said he had had enough of tenants with animals. He won't even allow pets. So, there are absolutely no cats here. If you really saw a cat, Gramps, it was probably not a cat but something else. It might not be an evil thing, but it's better not to get involved."

Shiina walked toward his own unit next door. He was a shady man, but it didn't seem like he had been lying.

"Grandpa . . ."

"I know, I know . . . but this thing is real."

Tatsuya took out the pink collar from his pocket, the

one the doctor had removed from the cat's neck. He clearly recalled the cat's warmth and weight. If that was indeed the cat on the flyer, he would not give up now.

Hayato was on his phone again and the two left the building. There was still no alley, and they emerged directly onto Fuyacho Street.

I need to find that building. The building with the strange clinic.

"Grandpa?"

"I know. You can go home. I know you have school at night."

"I think I found the cat."

"What?"

Hayato showed him his phone. Tatsuya put on his reading glasses and looked at the screen. There it was—the cat from the clinic. The way she was sitting with a look of disdain was exactly like in the photo on that flyer. She was even wearing a pink collar.

"What is this? How did you find it?"

"I searched on social media for tags related to lost cats. Apparently, she was found two months ago in Shiga Prefecture and was reported to the local police. I don't know if the person who found her still has her, but I'll send them a DM."

Tatsuya understood less than half of what Hayato had said, but he understood that the cat was taken in by someone in Shiga.

"Is the person's number on the post?"

"No number—but they've already responded. They said they still have the cat. To prevent fraud, they said, please contact the police or send them a photo. Huh, so that's how it works."

"A photo. Maybe I'll ask the Watanabes for one."

"I sent the picture of the flyer. I thought it'd be better not to lie unnecessarily, so I told them I spotted the cat on a flyer on the neighborhood bulletin board, which is the truth . . . Wait, I just got a reply. They say it is the cat. What do you think we should do, Grandpa?"

Tatsuya couldn't quite grasp the situation and didn't know how to answer Hayato's question.

"Wh-what do you think we should do?"

"We should contact the Watanabes and have them get in touch directly. From their DMs, they seem like nice people, so I think we can leave it to them to figure it out."

"Dee-ems?"

"Direct messages," said Hayato. It seemed like he had done everything he could, and he was respecting Tatsuya's wishes on what to do next.

Tatsuya thought it over. Indeed, it might be okay for them to step away now. The Watanabes were their neighbors, but they barely knew one another. It was bothersome and quite the hassle.

He also didn't know much about cats. Just that they could be large and warm. It wasn't like he wanted one as a pet or anything. If he was asked if he liked cats, he'd probably say no.

Whether he'd wanted to be bothered or hassled was his choice. He wasn't trapped in a locked cage; he was free. It was also true that he didn't much like cats. There was nothing wrong with that. He considered all these facts and made his decision.

"I'm going to confirm with my own eyes first, then let the Watanabes know."

"Okay, then I'll go with you. I'll ask the folks to let us visit the cat."

Hayato was quick to act. He informed the people who had the cat that they'd come over within the day.

— —

On the train ride to Shiga, Hayato showed Tatsuya the videos uploaded by the person caring for the cat. She was sprawled out like a rug, with several hands rubbing her belly. Just like the doctor mentioned, the cat's care-takers were indeed spoiling her.

"Someone from a cat rescue in Kyoto commented on this person's social media. They said if you find a lost cat, you should contact local animal control, the city authorities, or the police."

"But if you contact animal control, won't they take the cat away?"

"Apparently, if you report it as 'lost property,' you can hold on to it. The person from the rescue explained things very thoughtfully."

On Hayato's phone, Tatsuya saw that the comment was posted by someone named Kajiwara, the deputy director of the cat rescue. He wasn't used to reading on a screen and struggled with the tiny text. He kept adjusting his reading glasses back and forth, which made Hayato chuckle.

"If the owners of the lost cat had gotten in touch with local authorities, too, they might have connected faster. I bet the only thing the Watanabes did was to put up that flyer on the bulletin board. If they looked things up online, they'd have found people like this cat rescue guy who shares helpful information on finding lost cats."

"If I were the Watanabes, I would've only thought to

put flyers on the neighborhood bulletin board or on telephone poles, too."

"They only had their home phone number on that flyer, nothing else," said Hayato as he rested his cheek on his hand and gazed out the window.

They were on the local train heading east from Kyoto Station. From the window, they could see Lake Biwa. It was Tatsuya's first excursion in a long time.

To meet a cat with his grandson.

———

"Did you take that role in the neighborhood association?" asked Ayumi.

"I did."

Tatsuya sat with his arms crossed at the dining table covered in a mountain of paper, wondering where to begin. He had met with the association president and had been handed over these documents. In the aging neighborhood, there was a shortage of people who wanted to hold office, so Tatsuya was welcomed very warmly.

"I took the role, but I didn't think they would assign me three positions: chair of disaster prevention, vice treasurer, and local committee member. Well, I guess I'll just manage bit by bit."

"Oh my! Three positions?" Ayumi responded, her expression a complicated mix of happiness and concern.

"What if they digitized that stuff?"

When Tatsuya looked up, he saw Hayato sitting opposite him, his hair still messy from having just woken up. He was holding one of the files with faded papers.

"It's not like you ever look at this stuff. You can scan these to a digital archive and get rid of the paper."

"If we did whatever you just said, the older folks won't be able to keep up."

"Let's cut down on this culture of unnecessary paperwork for the next generation. We're not tossing out the old. We're just blending the old with the new."

"I can't make heads or tails of what you're saying."

Tatsuya was only half listening. Hayato smiled sleepily.

"I was thinking about that bulletin board from the other day and figured that a physical bulletin board is still pretty essential. There are still a lot of folks who aren't savvy with digital stuff. But if it was only the flyer, I don't think we'd have found Ms. Michiko. But if we'd relied solely on social media, we wouldn't have found the owners. So we really have to connect the two methods."

"Yeah, I still don't understand what you're saying."

"Just think of it as connecting you and me. We're working on a project at school about these kinds of innovations, so I'm going to use our neighborhood association as a model."

"I don't know what you're saying. Why are you taking that account book?"

"Okay, okay." Hayato laughed.

There was always a gap in language and sensibilities between generations. Sometimes, it was difficult to understand one another. Ayumi still half considered Hayato as a shut-in and was worried about Hayato and the nighttime walks he took with his grandfather, as she was worried about Tatsuya falling and injuring himself. Tatsuya, too, wasn't too keen on trying out new things.

But at seventy-eight, for the first time, he had experienced something truly baffling. The cat in Shiga was indeed the giant cat from the clinic. The mom from the family fostering Ms. Michiko brought her out like a big, heavy sack. The way the cat just dangled in the woman's arms, refusing to move while wearing a disdainful expression, was exactly the same.

Apparently, the family had been barbecuing by the shore of Lake Biwa when the kids found Ms. Michiko plodding around. She was wearing a collar, so they reported her to the police, but there was no coordinated effort to share information about lost pets across regions. In just a few days, the holding period for Ms. Michiko had been about to expire, and she was about to be adopted by the family who had found her.

The mom and kids had started to cry. They had grown fond of the cat. When Tatsuya showed them the pink collar, they were astonished—she had been wearing it until the day before. Since they had taken the cat in, they had not entrusted her to anyone else, and she had been lounging around the house the entire time. They had never heard of the clinic's name or address.

Everything seemed real, yet some of it felt like a dream. The foster mom seemed particularly curious about Nakagyō Kokoro Clinic for the Soul, and it seemed the rumor about the place was going to spread.

Would the door actually open when someone came by in the future? Would it open only if they were as desperate as the magnetic necklace guy?

The man had been shady, but he had also been kind in his own way. Tatsuya hoped that whoever came by after hearing the rumors would buy his necklaces.

Eventually, he planned to visit the Watanabes and

take a photo of Ms. Michiko. He wanted to send it to the family who had fostered her to let them know she was flourishing.

Meanwhile, Tatsuya was learning how to use his smartphone.

Shasha and Hajime

3

Shasha and Hajime

When Reona arrived home from school, she noticed it right away: her mother, standing in the kitchen, was looking unusually cheerful.

Oh no. Reona looked over her messages to her brother. They were marked as "read," but it seemed he hadn't contacted their mother.

"Mom?" she called out hesitantly.

Her mother was in the middle of coating shelled shrimp with batter.

"Oh, you're back. Tomoya will be back in a while, too, so let's wait a bit for dinner. I want to serve it nice and hot," she replied, her tone noticeably different.

The area next to the stove was crowded not just with shrimp but with a mountain of ingredients—vegetables and other seafood—ready to be fried. The fridge, too, was undoubtedly stocked with her brother's favorites.

Reona was irritated by her mother's overly cheerful mood, but she reluctantly broke the news.

"Tomoya's not coming tonight."

Her mother came rushing out from the kitchen. "Why?"

"Apparently, something came up at work."

"I've heard nothing about this."

Her mother's eyes narrowed in anger. But her ire was directed not at Reona's brother, who had broken his promise, but at Reona.

"Why didn't you tell me sooner? I already prepared dinner."

"Tomoya said he was going to get in touch with you."

"I haven't heard from him. If you knew, you could have just called me, Reona."

She had asked her brother to tell their mother himself because she knew how disappointed she would be. But now, it felt like she was being accused of keeping it from her.

If you're going to be mad, be mad with Tomoya. If Reona had said that aloud, she would only be adding fuel to the fire.

Her mother turned back toward the kitchen looking forlorn.

"What are we going to do with all this food?"

"We could just eat it," Reona suggested quietly.

Tomoya had begun living on his own in Kyoto a few years ago. New Year's was the only day you could count on him to come home. Otherwise, he visited once every six months at their mother's insistent urging. He was supposed to come by for dinner tonight, but something had come up at work. "Please let Mom know yourself," Reona had messaged, but he'd probably been too busy and had forgotten. Her brother was kind, but he was hopelessly careless.

Reona was twenty; her brother was twenty-nine. Due to their age difference, she had always perceived him as grown-up and mature. But now that she was older and they lived apart, she began to notice his unreliability, occasional thoughtlessness, and insensitivity. Sometimes, like he had done today, he would involve Reona in his communications with their parents. She suspected it had to do with the pressure he was feeling from their mother to visit home more frequently.

She was going to ask him to call their mother later, even if it was a bit of a hassle. Just hearing his voice would cheer her.

The soft tinkle of a bell. Hajime, the cat, was rubbing her head against the top of Reona's foot.

"All right, all right."

Reona stood still, patiently waiting for Hajime to finish nuzzling. The bell on her collar jingled softly. Hajime didn't enjoy being petted; she expressed affection by pressing her head against people's feet. Her entire body was covered in amber-colored stripes—even her eyes were a greenish amber. Fourteen years had passed since her brother had brought Hajime home as a kitten from his middle-school classmate's house. She used to have a glossier amber coat, but age had faded her fur to a yellowish shade reminiscent of a sun-bleached tatami mat, and her eyes had dulled to the color of its faded trim.

Hajime pressed her nose against Reona's palm. It was damp and cold.

"Hajime, you're just like our tatami mats."

Reona recalled visiting a pet shop recently with her friend Moé. There were no mixed-breed cats like Hajime there. Each one was cute as a plush toy, tumbling around in the display windows. They were all stylish kittens that would look out of place in an old house with only tatami rooms.

Hajime was nothing like them. Hajime was Hajime, and she was like no other cat. As soon as she was done nuzzling, she promptly headed off to the back room.

Reona's phone sounded. It was a message from her friend Shousuke.

"Mom, I'm going to eat later."

"What are you saying? You, too? Dinner's already ready."

"Sorry, you should eat without me. I'm going over to Shousuke's."

Ignoring her mother's protests, Reona left the house.

After walking for about ten minutes, she arrived at Shousuke Kunieda's house. She strode in without ringing the doorbell.

When she called out "Hello! It's Reona," Shousuke's mother emerged from the living room.

"Hi, Reona. He just got back from cram school a moment ago."

"Got it!"

Without knocking, Reona went into his room upstairs. Shousuke sat cross-legged on the floor, his back to her.

"What's the emergency? Did you snag a rare character toy at the arcade?"

Shousuke ignored her. Reona rummaged through his bookshelf, searching for a manga she hadn't read yet.

"You don't have any new releases. What's up? I gave up fried shrimp to be here. Not that the shrimp was meant for me."

At least half of Shousuke's bookshelf was filled with college entrance exam prep books, all worn-out from heavy use. Shousuke, Reona's childhood friend and the same age, was in his third year of trying for Kyoto University. He had taken the exam the first year with no expectations, believing the second year would be his serious attempt. But that had ended in failure, too, and this winter, he was preparing to face the exam for a third time.

He kept his back to her. In the past, when he turned away from her like this, he'd be facing his desk. He hadn't ever brushed Reona off when she dropped by, but he would continue to study as they talked. But recently, he'd been spending more time gaming and reading comics. Sometimes, she'd find him just lounging around. He still attended cram school, but there was a visible decline in his pace. But he was probably most aware of that himself. Reona continued making mundane small talk, careful not to put any undue pressure on her friend.

"Honestly, my mom is way too obsessed with my

brother. When he can't come home, she flips out on *me*. I guess it can't be helped. At least cats don't care about human schedules or relationships."

"*Cats?*" Shousuke responded, still turned away from her.

"Yeah. You know my brother works for that cat rescue center in Minami Ward. He's super busy with the intake and placement of cats. Even though he's the center's deputy director, he says he's basically just an errand boy."

"He's probably lying." Shousuke's voice carried a mix of laughter, disbelief, and a hint of mockery.

His comment instantly riled her. Her brother was not the type to lie and avoid coming home. If anything, she wished he *would* lie and come up with a better cover for once. Shousuke, who was an old friend, should know that much.

"What do you mean? If it wasn't work, why—" Reona started to retort but stopped short when she noticed something: a slender strand resembling a piece of fluffy twine swaying in Shousuke's lap.

"*Wait a second!*"

She leaped around him. Nestled between his crossed legs was a bundle of fine, grayish-brown fur.

"No *way*! What is it?"

"It's a cat."

"Yes, I *get* that. I mean . . ."

Reona gasped. A tiny cat was facing her. Its eyes were almost perfect circles and were a dusty shade of baby blue. If she remembered correctly, that distinctive eye color was known as "kitten blue"—a nervous shade of blue. The cat was trying clumsily to crawl out of Shousuke's lap. It extended its short legs earnestly but kept missing.

"So adorable." Overwhelmed by the sheer cuteness, Reona's eyes crinkled and her voice melted. "Is that a Munchkin?"

"Looks like it," Shousuke replied, handing her a piece of paper. She took it and read aloud.

"*Name: Shasha. Female. Two months old. Munchkin. Feed moderate amounts of cat food in the morning and at night. Water bowl must always be full. Clean kitty litter as needed. This is a crucial time for her development. She will grow by cultivating curiosity and trying new things. She may engage in reckless play, so please watch out for risky behavior, such as jumping from high places, swallowing objects, and other accidents. Please keep her indoors. That's all.* What is this about?"

"It's an instruction manual for the cat. They gave it

to me along with a bunch of other things," Shousuke said, glancing at the bowls, bag of cat food, and other essentials for raising a cat.

They were all things never seen before in this room she had been frequenting since childhood.

Shousuke had always enjoyed studying, and his grades had been stellar. They were both twenty now, yet remained very close. Whenever they faced problems, they talked to each other, and they maintained their bond through his entrance exam failures and his disappointment over having to take a gap year.

And now, this Shousuke had brought home a cat. The Munchkin, with its short legs and petite stature, was a popular breed. If you were to pick a cat by its cuteness, this one would rank high. But had he considered things thoroughly?

Cats were not all the same. Care, characteristics, and lifespan varied from breed to breed. If he'd consulted her beforehand, what advice would she have given him? But she didn't want to find fault with the kitten that was already there.

"This is most definitely an emergency," Reona said in a deliberately casual tone. "I'm sure it's not the case, but you didn't just impulsively pick up the cat, did you?"

"Not at all," he said. "It was prescribed to me at a clinic."

He looked down at the cat with a worried smile. To prevent her from escaping his crossed legs, he raised his knees and tried to block her with his thighs.

It took a moment for Reona, who had been distracted by the cat's cute gestures, to register Shousuke's words.

"Wait, what did you just say?"

"It was prescribed."

"What was?"

"The cat."

"By whom?"

"Tomoya. Man, something's up with your brother. He was there, in this old building in a back alley in Nakagyō. It was pretty . . . intense."

Something's up with my brother?

As Reona watched the cat clambering up Shousuke's legs, she recalled how her friend Moé had also recently mentioned wandering into an alley in Nakagyō.

⸺ ◦ ⸺

The next day, Reona visited Shousuke at his place again. It was already nine thirty at night, a time when most people would hesitate to drop by someone's house.

She did figure that the front door would be locked, so she'd reached out to him ahead of time. Outside his house, she dialed his number, and the door opened before the call connected.

"It's late. Coming back from work at Nanzen-ji?"

"Yeah. It was super busy today. Why is boiled tofu so popular? It's delicious, sure, but can't you get it in other prefectures?"

"Eating it in Kyoto has a certain charm to it."

As they chatted on their way to the second floor, Shou-suke's mother stuck her head out from the living room.

"Welcome, Reona. Shousuke, it's late, so make sure you walk her home later."

"I will!"

As soon as they reached Shousuke's room, Reona started looking around for the cat.

"Where is she?"

"In that cardboard box."

Shousuke pointed at a tiny box, one that might be used to ship cosmetics. She peered inside—the cat was fast asleep on her back, belly exposed.

"She's asleep."

"Yup."

"She's in deep sleep mode."

"Super deep sleep mode."

The cat had contorted her body like a child sleeping restlessly, with her paws thrown above her head. But with her short legs, she looked rather silly. Reona had been hoping to play, but she couldn't bring herself to wake her up, seeing how blissfully she slept.

"I'm not here to see the cat." Reona wrenched herself away from the cardboard box. "So, I went looking for the clinic after class."

"Did you see your brother there? Wasn't he over-the-top cheerful?"

It seemed he truly believed that his friend's kind older brother had somehow turned into a sketchy back-alley doctor.

Reona hadn't immediately dismissed Shousuke's story either. And, just like the time she had gone with Moé, she still hadn't been able to locate the clinic.

"I didn't find it: the building or the clinic. And I called my brother, but we were only able to chat for a short while because he had to take a bunch of cats to get vaccinated or something. He barely has time to eat. There's no way he has a side hustle, much less as a doctor. Impossible!"

"But it was one hundred percent your brother."

"Shousuke, you've known my brother for years. You know that his inoffensive face is a dime a dozen."

Shousuke laughed. "That's not very nice."

Reona's brother, Tomoya, had a lean build and a kindly face, but there was nothing special or memorable about his looks.

Shousuke had bigger eyes and chiseled features. He was no Adonis, but she thought he was cute. But he had lost a remarkable amount of weight over the past six months.

She knew that spending a gap year studying for exams must be tough, but instead of pointing out the obvious, she thought it would be better to bring some levity to the situation. Just when she was about to bad-mouth her brother to lighten the mood, the cardboard box began to rustle.

"Hey, is the cat awake?"

"Looks like it."

Just as Reona was about to reach into the box, it tipped over. A grayish-brown bundle of fur, wrapped in a towel, toppled out.

"Uh-oh, she got out."

"This one's super energetic. While she's awake, she never sits still."

She was tumbling back and forth, her claws stuck in the towel. She was cute, but she was clearly a handful.

"What did you do with her today? Did you have your mom look after her?"

"No, no. I attended online classes at home today, so I was able to keep an eye on her. Honestly, I spent most of my time playing with her instead of studying." Shousuke gazed at the kitten, his eyes softening. It seemed the cat was some sort of wonder cure.

"She's so tiny but fearless. Look."

Shasha clumsily scrambled toward the bed. She tried to leap onto the sheets, but, missing her mark, she flopped onto the floor. But she didn't give up, jumping again, only to fall over once more. Reona grinned, but after seeing her flip over several times, she became worried.

"Is that safe?"

"It's fine. Just watch."

The cat braced her short legs and took a tiny hop. But alas, she still couldn't reach the bed.

"Go, Shasha, go!" Shousuke pumped his fist to cheer her on.

"You got this, Shasha!" said Reona.

Shasha's claws finally caught, and she began to scale the sheets.

"Yay! Good job, Shasha!"

"This one'll keep trying until she succeeds. Yesterday, it was a stack of books she tried to get up on. Earlier, it was my backpack. She's always aiming for higher and higher places. Cats grow up so quickly, you know. Things she couldn't do yesterday, she can do today. The more she practices, the higher she can jump."

"I see," Reona said with a nod, thinking Shousuke likely saw himself in the cat. He was also growing from his challenges and, like the fearless and tenacious Shasha, he was determined to give his all until he passed his university entrance exams.

"Reona, I'm going to give up on Kyoto University."

"*What?*"

Reona froze, the smile still on her face. Shousuke gave a thin smile in return.

"The truth is, I've been struggling for a while now. I couldn't give up, I just kept jumping at it like Shasha. But see how she's learning to leap higher and higher? Me, on the other hand . . . I was never within reaching distance from the start. No matter how many times I jumped, I couldn't get any closer. I've known this all along, but I didn't know how to stop. I just wanted someone to tell me to give up already. That's why I ended up at your brother's . . . weird clinic. And, well, here I am with this cat."

Shousuke scooped up the cat, who had joined them on top of the bed.

"This cat works precisely, so I only have her for three days. I need to return her tomorrow."

"Oh? You're not keeping her?"

"No." Shousuke paused for a moment before he continued. "I haven't given up on college entirely. There's a private college with a program I want to pursue. I'll have to convince my parents to let me shift the direction of my studies, and it'll require even more work on my part. If I had an adorable cat like this one around, I'd never focus. I can't bring a cat home knowing I wouldn't be able to take care of it, right?"

Shousuke touched his nose to Shasha's. "It's cold!" he said. He turned away and pressed his forehead against the cat's. "Giving up isn't the same as running away. It takes courage to let go of unreachable goals and leap toward something new." He closed his eyes. "Both you and I have courage," he said to Shasha.

"I see."

That was all Reona could say. A childhood friend who had moved on. A kitten she thought she would watch grow. Suddenly, she felt as if she were the only one left behind. Then, a thought struck her.

"You're going to the clinic tomorrow?"

"Yeah."

"I'm coming with you!"

A peculiar clinic with a doctor that her friend insisted looks just like her brother. Both Moé and Shousuke had been able to find the clinic; she felt frustrated that she was the only one who couldn't.

"I'm definitely going with you!"

"Okay, okay," said Shousuke.

The cat dozed off in his hands.

———— × ————

As soon as classes were over, Reona dashed off campus. She had already switched her shift at work. Her plan was to head directly to Shousuke's house and travel to the clinic together with Shousuke and the cat. Her heart was racing. She had the feeling that something extraordinary was about to happen.

But when she saw her phone, she looked up to the heavens in exasperation. There was a message from her brother. *You have got to be kidding*, she thought. He was coming by the house that night.

Not that she wasn't glad, but when her brother came home, their mother insisted on having a family dinner. Only their father could be excused from attending if he was busy with work.

Why today of all days? In the first place, I don't need to be there. As long as my brother's there, it's all that matters. As soon as her brother arrived, she'd eat her dinner in a hurry, then leave.

When she got home that night, Tomoya was already there. He sat in the living room, typing away on a laptop. It was unusual for him to drop by before finishing work.

"Hey, you're here early. It's only five o'clock."

"I was picking up donations of supplies nearby. Since I had to suddenly cancel plans the other day, I thought I'd show my face, even for a little bit, today."

"Oh, that's unusually thoughtful of you."

"What do you mean *unusually*?"

Tomoya wore a gentle smile. His jacket was covered in dust, and his hair was overgrown. When she had last seen him six months ago, he had looked more trim. He must have been swamped. She couldn't complain about his last-minute cancellation the other day or his unexpected visit today. In any case, whenever she criticized her brother, their mother would annoyingly defend him. But today, there was no one in the kitchen.

"Where's Mom?"

"Well, actually, she ran off to the market. I told her I can't stay long, but she insisted I eat before I leave. She went to buy sushi." Tomoya smiled thinly.

You can get fresh sushi anywhere these days! Reona was fed up with their mother, who would do anything to keep her brother from leaving. When it came to her brother, their mother was constantly spinning her wheels alone.

A chime sounded, and Hajime peeked her head out from the tatami room in the back. Her tiny ears were perked up, and her light brown eyes were wide.

"Hey, Hajime. How's it going?" Tomoya called out.

Hajime froze in her tracks. She stared at Tomoya with the sharp glare of an alley cat before retreating to the back room.

Tomoya chuckled. "Still frosty as ever."

Hajime had never liked men—she'd never taken to Tomoya or their father. Their father had long given up on winning Hajime's affection and now largely ignored her. Tomoya always stooped down low to speak to the cat, but Hajime continued to give him the cold shoulder.

Reona would have felt heartbroken if the cat she'd brought didn't warm up to her. Yet her brother never showed any signs of being upset, and when he lived at home, he'd never once forgotten to feed her. Cats were simply not animals swayed by a sense of obligation or emotion, and no matter how much you did for them, they only showed affection to the people they chose. Even though Tomoya was the most familiar with cats, Hajime always treated him coldly.

But surely, Tomoya's love reached his own cat, the one he had in his apartment.

"How's little Nikké?"

"He's always asleep. It's been a while since I've seen him awake."

"Really? Hajime has been sleeping a lot, too. I guess she's getting old."

"Is she eating?"

"Yes, but slowly. We give her soft food for senior cats."

"Wet food can spoil pretty fast, so it's a good idea to serve it in smaller portions and throw out anything she doesn't finish. I know school keeps you super busy, but try to keep an eye on her food."

"Got it."

Her brother was always mild natured, and time seemed to move slowly around him. Just talking to him made her feel calm.

Tomoya's phone beeped. After glancing at the message, he gave a soft sigh.

"It's Mom. She says it's really busy at the supermarket, and she's going to be back late."

"Of course it's busy—it's the evening."

"Right." Tomoya shifted uneasily. It seemed he wanted to leave.

"If you have to be somewhere, you should tell Mom."

"I don't need to be anywhere. It's just— No, I can't. It wouldn't make sense to leave after coming all this way. I'll leave after dinner," he said, sounding like he had just made an important decision. Time moved slowly around Tomoya, but sometimes *he* was the slow one.

Now that she knew her mother would be home late, Reona decided not to wait any longer. They'd probably fight about this later, but she didn't care.

"I'm going out with Shousuke now. Mom's fine as long as you're here. Do you mind if I go?"

"A date with Shousuke? You guys have always been close. Sure, go ahead."

"Thanks. But it's not a date." Reona laughed. "You

have to keep this a secret, but we're going to a mental health clinic—Kokoro Clinic for the Soul or something. Shousuke's a bit worn-out from the college exam stress. Have you heard about this place somewhere around Fuyacho Street? It's a bizarre clinic that prescribes cats."

"Prescribes cats?" asked Tomoya, tilting his head slightly.

"Yup. I couldn't tell Shousuke this, but I think it's kind of questionable that they loan out cats. What do you think?"

"Are you talking about Dr. Kokoro's practice?" Tomoya gave a faint smile. "It's not a mental health clinic, but it certainly has cats. Tell Shousuke he's welcome to drop by the rescue center anytime if he wants to play with cats. We have cats we're trying to socialize and chubby cats that could use some exercise."

"Hmm. Okay." Reona felt like they weren't entirely on the same page, but still, it seemed like even her brother knew about that odd clinic in Nakagyō Ward. Apparently, this Dr. Kokoro was rather well-known.

When she arrived at Shousuke's place, she found him home from cram school and waiting for her. Shasha was already inside her pet carrier. Reona offered to carry the carrier, and together, they made their way to the clinic.

"Thanks for being there yesterday when I spoke to my parents about my college plans," said Shousuke.

"No problem. And your parents didn't seem that surprised."

"Well, I've failed the entrance exams twice already. The school I'm considering now is in a different prefecture, and if I get in, I'll need to live in a dorm. They're a bit exasperated by how much it'll all cost."

"But your parents care about you so much. In my family, everyone is always fussing over my brother, while I'm pretty much on my own. I chose my college myself, and no one pays any mind when I come home late from work. Your mom is so much more caring—she's always worried about me getting home safely."

"Old-fashioned parents are like that. It's got nothing to do with you. Even I can see that Tomoya's a bit out of touch with the real world, so I get why they worry. I bet he's popular with the ladies. He's the kind of guy who triggers maternal instincts."

"As a sister, that's something I'd rather not think about. Ugh, it gives me the creeps!"

Reona's brother was single, and she had no idea if he was even seeing anyone. Given his preoccupation with animals, she had a feeling he was oblivious to romance.

He would probably care more about the cats than his girlfriend.

"Watch your feet," said Shousuke. "There's a ledge there."

"Huh?"

When she looked down, she saw her feet caught on the low step of an entrance. Without her knowing, they had arrived at a long and narrow building. A dimly lit hallway stretched out before them. Reona stared blankly.

"This is the place?"

"Yup."

"When did we get here?"

"What are you talking about? You're weird. Let's go."

She followed Shousuke and discovered that there was indeed a clinic on the fifth floor. Inside, it was neat and sparsely furnished, with a nurse sitting at the reception window.

"Mr. Kunieda, you're here to return the cat, right? The doctor is waiting for you. Please head in."

The nurse seemed like a forceful personality. She did not look at Reona. Typically, only the patient was permitted in the examination room, but she had come all that way and wanted to meet the strange doctor who prescribed cats.

"Excuse me," Reona addressed the nurse. "I'm a friend of the patient. May I go in with him?"

The nurse looked up. "Are you a patient?"

"No, I'm not. I'm just here with my friend."

"You're a patient, I see," the nurse said, ignoring Reona's protest. "In that case, go right ahead. The doctor is waiting for you."

What a charmless woman. Shousuke entered the examination room, and Reona trailed behind, carrying the cat carrier. The room contained just two plain chairs and a desk with a computer. It was so compact that their presence made the space feel cramped.

"It's tight in here, isn't it? Is this normal for an examination room? We're practically nose to nose."

"I agree. It's my first time at a psychiatric clinic, but I have to say this place is full of odd quirks," said Shousuke as he settled into a chair.

Reona remained standing with the cat carrier in her arms, her back pressed against the wall. She surveyed her surroundings. So, this was Dr. Kokoro's office. Not only was it small, there was no medical equipment. It was merely a space for conversation.

"Huh."

"What's up? You seem unhappy."

"Not really. I was just wondering why you didn't talk to me before seeing a doctor. I had no idea you were feeling so desperate."

"Well, I figured you'd just get angry at me and tell me to stop moping around." Shousuke made it seem as though she had been insensitive. Just as she was about to reply, a man in a white lab coat walked into the room.

"Hello, Mr. Kunieda. Ah, you look well. It seems the cat was rather effective. How splendid." The doctor smiled as he lowered himself into his chair and turned his gaze toward Reona. "Oh, dear, we can't ignore this one, can we?"

"To—"

Tomoya!

She barely caught herself, her cheeks twitching with shock.

It was more than just a resemblance. The man before her was the spitting image of her brother. It was no wonder Shousuke confused them. Everything—his physique, facial features, skin texture and color, and even his voice—was exactly the same.

But it wasn't him. His mannerisms weren't like her brother's at all. Tomoya would never giggle foolishly like this doctor, nor would he speak in such an oddly old-fashioned way. The contrast felt even more pronounced since she had just seen him at home. He was undeniably a different person. Yet, it was unsettling how closely they resembled each other.

The doctor gave Reona a concerned look. "Hmm? What's wrong? Your cheeks are jumping up and down."

"They're twitching," she snapped. She found it irritating that someone who looked so much like Tomoya was teasing her.

"Is that so?" The doctor chuckled. "Now, how did it go for you, Mr. Kunieda? Did anyone tell you that it's okay if you give up?"

"No." Shousuke shook his head. "I said it to myself."

"I see. That's good to hear. If you want something said, it's fastest to say it yourself. It's more accurate, too. But when you find yourself at a loss for words, that's when you get a cat to lend you a paw. A cat punch will knock some sense into you. Well, take care." The doctor turned to Reona. "Well, then. It's your first time at our clinic, isn't it? What's your name and age?"

"Um," said Reona. "Reona Kajiwara. I'm twenty years old."

"What brings you in today?"

"There's nothing wrong with me. I'm just here accompanying this cat."

Reona pushed the cat carrier toward the doctor, but he nudged it back toward her.

"If you want something said, it's fastest to say it yourself. It's more accurate, too."

Was he repeating himself now? Reona felt irritated by the doctor's insinuation that she was harboring issues.

"I don't have anything I want said."

The doctor stood up and brought his face alarmingly close to hers.

"Hmm. It seems you've been taking a cat for a while, but you're a bit too dependent on it. Of course, cats are excellent for household harmony, but it's not good to be too reliant on them. You need to be a bit more independent."

Is he referring to Hajime? How does he know about her?

Reona was beyond creeped out, even fearful. This doctor looked too much like Tomoya to be a coincidence. It felt as if her usually serious brother was playing a prank on her, and it sent a chill down her spine.

She tightened her grip on the pet carrier. *I'm going to return her, then leave.*

But before she could react, the doctor leaned in even closer, smiling calmly.

"What brings you in today?"

He's way too close. He was like a cat pressing its damp nose against her. He was so near that her eyes couldn't focus. The tip of the doctor's nose and his eyes swam in a blur.

Nothing. Nothing's wrong. But in a daze, she blurted, "I think I hate my mom."

She was shocked by the words that had slipped out.

What did I just say?

Her own teen-rebellion-like outburst made Reona break out in a cold sweat. Declaring you hated your mom was something a grade-schooler would do. She uncomfortably avoided the doctor's eyes as he offered a comforting smile.

"Is that true?"

Reona shook her head in denial. "No, it's not. Ignore what I just said. Pretend you didn't hear anything."

The doctor's smile widened. "My hearing is excellent, so it's impossible for me to pretend I didn't hear anything. Well then, Ms. Kajiwara, we'll prescribe you a cat. Hmm. How about the one in the carrier?"

"Huh?" Reona looked down at the carrier. "Shasha?"

"Yes. She's conveniently right there. It'll be great."

"Hold on a moment," Reona interjected, her tone sharper than before as she regarded the doctor. "Isn't it awful to treat the cat as if she's an object? 'She's conveniently right there.' In the first place, even if this is a psychiatric clinic, I can't imagine how stressful it must be for the cat to be loaned out to strangers."

"It's a common misunderstanding, but this is not a psychiatric clinic. Cats aren't meant to be borrowed or loaned. If I tried that, they'd scratch me. They are all very strong-willed. Isn't that right?"

The doctor lowered his head and peeked into the carrier, but Shasha didn't react.

"Ah, playing the cat, are we? You're quite the performer for being so small. Cats build their own worlds, whether they're locked in a small cage or roaming under the expansive sky. That domain belongs solely to them; outsiders cannot intrude. Unless they invite you in, you can't enter. Like a door bolted shut." The doctor nodded, visibly pleased with himself.

Reona had been listening in puzzlement. *What nonsense. What is it that he actually wants to say?*

"Well, I'd like you to consider the stress on the cat as well."

The doctor chuckled. "The cats work extra well on people like you who care. I'm going to prescribe you this cat. Don't forget to take it with the cat you already have. It'll be a double-dose attack on your ailment," the doctor announced, sounding as if he were selling a combination cold medicine in a commercial. He burst into another fit of giggles.

Shousuke spoke in a whisper to Reona. "Are you okay? This is all really odd."

"Yeah. A double-dose attack?"

"No, not that." Shousuke hesitated. "The thing about hating your mom."

"Ah, no, no, no!" Her face turned scarlet in an instant. *Shoot. I need Shousuke to pretend he didn't hear anything either.* She was so embarrassed, she couldn't look him in the eye. "It's not true. Don't take it seriously."

Shousuke nodded and smiled awkwardly. "Got it."

What's gotten into me? Had she been thrown off because the doctor looked identical to her brother?

Sure, some aspects of her mother irritated her, but voicing those feelings out loud made them seem much harsher. Feeling annoyed with someone is completely different from hating them.

"We'll prescribe you the cat for ten days. I'll write

you a prescription, so please pick up what you need from reception."

"Ten days?" asked Shousuke. "Won't Shasha's owner worry if she's gone for that long?"

"Not to worry. This one doesn't have an owner yet. Someone took her from a breeder, but they returned her when they found another cat they preferred. It happens quite often. It's no bad thing to be choosey about your cat, whether it be about its appearance or breed. It's a long-term relationship, after all. There's no way of knowing if your choice might end up changing something for someone down the line, is there?"

What on earth did he mean?

As she listened to the doctor, a haze of discontent settled over her. She could feel the cat's warmth through the carrier. It seemed too cruel that such an adorable kitten had been returned.

"All right, that's it for today. We're closing up, and I'm running out of energy. If you're able to say what you want to say before the ten-day dose is up, you're welcome to bring the cat back early."

Forcibly ushered out by the smiling doctor, the two left the examination room with the pet carrier they had arrived with. Reona and Shousuke exchanged glances.

"I guess you got prescribed a cat, too."

"Yeah . . . That wasn't my intention."

"What are you going to do? You already have a cat at home, right?"

"Hajime's mild and quite old, so I don't think she'll pick a fight with the kitten."

Reona was perplexed. She'd never imagined that she, too, would be prescribed a cat.

Until now, she had never let any cat other than Hajime into her home. And Hajime, too, had never left the house except for the one time she had to go to the vet for her vaccinations; she was ignorant to the ways of the world and other cats. Reona had no idea how she would react to Shasha.

"Ms. Kajiwara?" The nurse waved from the reception window.

Reona handed over the prescription and received a paper bag in return.

"Here are your supplies. There's an instruction leaflet inside, which I advise you to read carefully."

"I'll carry it," offered Shousuke. He took the bag and pulled out the leaflet. They read it together.

"*Name: Shasha. Female. Two months old. Munchkin. Feed moderate amounts of cat food in the morning and at night. Water bowl must always be full. Clean kitty litter as needed. This is a crucial time for developing social skills. Play-fighting with siblings will teach her about pain and restraint. It's important she learns this so she doesn't accidentally injure others when she's older. Please keep her indoors. That's all."*

It had said something similar in the leaflet Shousuke had received previously. For a cat owner, the instructions weren't particularly useful. The bag contained only the bare essentials necessary to raise a cat.

It was such an unexpected turn of events, and Reona's frustration grew at the clinic's negligence. The doctor talked a lot about cats' worlds, but wasn't he essentially just shifting the responsibility of their care onto the patients? If the person entrusted with the cat was unreliable, it was only the cat who would pay the price.

She knew she was stubborn, but she confronted the nurse anyway. "Don't you think it's a bit careless to be leaving cats in people's care? Shasha is only two months old, and there should be many more instructions and precautions listed in the leaflet."

"Please look up that information yourself. Now, take care."

The nurse didn't even glance up.

So unpleasant, thought Reona.

"I have a cat, so I generally know what to do. But that guy over there, he doesn't know anything about cats and received exactly the same basic instruction leaflet. That's awful."

"Whether you do your own research on your prescription or follow the doctor's orders really depends on the person, doesn't it?"

"You're absolutely right," murmured Shousuke from behind.

Reona shot him a sharp glare, but he pretended not to notice. She knew he was siding with the nurse because she was pretty.

The doctor is weird. The nurse is arrogant. I would've been better off not finding the clinic at all.

"Fine! I have a brother who works at a cat rescue, so I can ask him if I have any questions. My brother is very knowledgeable about cats. He's an expert and super reliable."

"Is that right? Well, as the doctor said just now, as soon as you're able to say what you want to say, you can bring the cat back."

"I don't—"

"Take care."

"What is with you?"

"Take care."

No matter how forcefully Reona spoke, the nurse remained unfazed.

As they left the clinic, Shousuke smirked. "It's the first time I've seen you lose an argument."

"That nurse makes me so mad!"

The pet carrier jiggled.

"Oh, sorry! I'm not mad at you, Shasha. I'm angry with everyone but you—the doctor, the nurse, myself, Shousuke."

"Me, too? Well, I guess I started it all. But it's probably good that you came to the clinic with me. It feels like you were meant to come."

"Not true. I don't even know why I said what I said just now."

Reona fell silent. Shousuke didn't press further.

"What about the cat? If it's too much for you, I can look after her at my place."

"No, it's fine. She was prescribed to me, so I'll take care of her at my place. I won't pass her off."

"But won't your parents mind?"

"Don't worry. I have a plan."

Reona wasn't concerned about her father, who simply wasn't interested in cats. The real challenge was her fusspot mother. Clutching the pet carrier close to her chest, Reona turned to Shousuke.

"Thanks for walking me home. Don't worry about Shasha."

"If things don't work out, call me. You can leave her at my place."

"It'll be fine. I just checked—my brother's back at his apartment."

She saw Shousuke off, then stepped into her house. Her father wasn't home yet, and her mother was washing dishes in the kitchen. She appeared to be in a good mood, but the moment she saw Reona, her face crunched into a scowl.

"Really, you are too much! Tomoya made a rare visit home, and you just go off somewhere. That was so insensitive of you."

I have plans, too, you know! Reona would usually have snapped back at her mother, but today, she left it. She felt guilty for having declared she hated her mom, even if she hadn't said it directly to her.

"I had plans with Shousuke from before."

"Oh, Shousuke. I'm sure he's having a tough time

with exams, but life is even harder in the real world. Just look at Tomoya—he didn't have to work at such a demanding place like the cat rescue center. Tomoya's such a sensitive boy, so I'm sure he's going through a lot."

Tomoya. It was always Tomoya with her mother. She always found a way to bring him up. This, too, would have normally irritated Reona, but today, she couldn't help but smile at how everything was going as she had expected.

She set the carrier on the floor. She had only ten days with the cat and didn't want to spend that time arguing. She opened the carrier door and gently pulled the kitten out.

Shasha truly resembled a fur ball. Perhaps she was feeling nervous, as her fur was fluffed up as if charged with static. Her ash-blue eyes were wide with bewilderment. Her forepaws, resting in Reona's hands, looked like a baby's clenched fists.

"Oh, dear." Her mother, too, looked bewildered. "What is that?"

"Cute, right? It's a Munchkin, a popular breed."

"No, I mean, where did you get it from? How could you when we have Hajime?"

Rather than anger or outright refusal, her mother displayed confusion.

Reona pressed her nose against Shasha's. "Do you think it'll be a problem? Will Hajime be upset?"

"Of course!" snapped her mother. "She'll be surprised by the sudden appearance of another cat."

"I guess it can't be helped, then. I'll take her back to Tomoya."

"What?" Her mother's voice changed.

"This cat's from Tomoya's cat rescue. I only have her for ten days before her new owner picks her up. But since she's little and needs lots of care, he asked me to look after her."

"Oh, I see. If that's the case, then . . ."

"I guess it won't work. I'll talk to Tomoya and tell him to come take her—"

"Wait, what are you saying? Tomoya already has a cat at his place, and he's swamped with work. Why don't we just keep her here? Such a small kitten . . . No, no, Tomoya can't handle her."

"Really?"

It was just as Reona had expected. Her mother inadvertently redirected her anger toward her in support of

Tomoya. Typically, this would have irked her, but today, it made her smile.

Her mother observed Shasha from a distance.

"She's like a stuffed animal. I wonder if Hajime will get jealous."

"If Hajime doesn't like her, just keep them apart. Shasha can stay in my room."

Sensing a presence, Reona turned around. Hajime was peering at her from the gap between the sliding doors. Her black pupils were sharp like knives, and her yellow-green irises were narrowed.

Cats are inscrutable. Unlike humans, the corners of their mouths don't curve into a smile, and their eyes don't turn into half-moons when they are happy. Yet, after living with her for fourteen years, Reona could read Hajime so well.

She entered the living room in silence, taking careful steps, her tail held high and gently swaying from side to side.

In an instant, Shasha was thrashing wildly in Reona's hands, trying to get down. But Reona held her tightly. Shasha was a naïve little kitten, believing that the other cat would welcome her. Even calm Hajime would not be so pleased if Shasha suddenly pounced on her. It was crucial not to get Hajime on the offensive.

Hajime drew closer, sniffing, nose in the air, as she circled Reona, who was now crouching. She leaned in toward Shasha and began poking her with her snout. Shasha twitched restlessly in response.

"Shasha, hold still. Hajime hasn't finished checking you out."

"That's right, little kitty. Hajime's inspections are thorough."

Mother and daughter bent their heads together nervously toward the cats as they interacted. Hajime pressed her head against Reona's side and began sniffing Shasha's behind. Shasha flapped her short legs.

"Oh, dear, how embarrassing, little kitty! She's sniffing your butt."

Reona's mother laughed.

After thoroughly sniffing Shasha's butt, Hajime sat down on the tatami as if to say, "That's enough."

"Is Hajime done with her inspection?"

"Looks like it. Seems like the kitty passed."

Reona set Shasha down on the tatami. The kitten bounded over to Hajime and began prodding her with her front legs, evidently wanting to sniff Hajime's butt like she had done hers earlier.

But Hajime's behind was planted firmly on the floor, leaving no gap. And because her coat matched the light brown of the tatami, it almost seemed as though she had grown out of the floor itself. Still, Shasha didn't give up and continued to sniff around where Hajime's butt met the tatami. Hajime remained poker-faced.

"Hajime's completely ignoring her."

Reona held in her laughter. Her mother was also smirking.

Suddenly, Hajime stood up and began chasing Shasha's tail. Shasha, not wanting to have her butt sniffed, darted away, but she couldn't outrun Hajime. Hajime nudged Shasha from behind with her nose, and Shasha's legs lifted into the air.

"Oh, dear, kitty, you got your bottom sniffed again. How embarrassing."

"Come on, Shasha! You got this! Don't lose the battle of bottoms!"

"Look, here comes Hajime again. She's coming in for a sniff!"

"Ah, look, this is your chance, Shasha! Hajime is doing the flehmen response!"

Reona and her mother watched the two cats circle each other. Reona's face was in a permanent grin.

It was an overwhelming victory for Hajime in that night's battle of the bottoms. She didn't have her butt sniffed even once.

— · —

How many times had she carried the generously filled clay pots to the tables?

When the cherry blossoms began to bud, the number of tourists in Kyoto surged. The same happened when the leaves changed color. All the eateries around Nanzen-ji Temple were packed with people waiting for seats, and the boiled tofu restaurant where Reona worked also had a wait of several hours.

Reona rushed to the restaurant after class, put on her uniform kimono, and commenced working tirelessly until eight p.m. Her primary responsibility was serving tables, but she also took it upon herself to handle the heavy lifting, which included clay pots and cases of beer.

During a brief break, Reona finally found a chance to use the bathroom. She had been holding it in for hours. A coworker rushed into the bathroom with her.

"That was close. One day, I'm going to pee my pants in front of the customers."

"Me, too. I just barely made it," said Reona, adjusting the sleeves of her kimono. She'd been working part-time at this restaurant for two years, and it was always like this during the super busy season.

Her coworker let out a heavy sigh. Her kimono was wrinkled, perhaps from also working long hours without breaks.

"I had no days off this week, and I have shifts all weekend, too. How about you, Reona?"

"I have a few days off starting tomorrow."

"Really? Exam week at school?"

"I have a cat over."

"A cat?"

"Just for a few days. A Munchkin kitten. She is unbelievably adorable."

"A kitten!" Her coworker let out a groan. "Definitely not the time to be working. I have a cat at home, too, and kittens grow up so quickly. You can't miss this moment. Go home early. There's just some cleaning left, and I can take care of it."

"Thank you."

The cat effect is powerful. Reona couldn't help but

laugh. But indeed, it was a rare opportunity to be able to interact with a kitten. Because she had swapped yesterday's shift, she couldn't take the day off today, but she planned to stay at home as much as possible while Shasha was there. She helped quickly with the cleanup and rushed home.

———

"Where's Shasha?" asked Reona, panting as she tossed her shoes aside.

Her mother laughed. "She's already asleep in the back room. It's already nine o'clock."

"Ugh, I rushed home!"

She stepped into the tatami room, leaving the lights off. Though Hajime slept in different spots throughout the house, depending on her mood, this was the room she slept in the most. Had she given it up to Shasha tonight?

There was a single cushion in the corner. Hajime lay atop it, her back toward the room. Reona looked around for Shasha but couldn't find her. There was no way she could have gotten on top of the cabinet. There was nowhere to hide. As she went farther into the room, she spotted something grayish-brown and fluffy beside Hajime.

It was Shasha. Both cats were asleep, facing each other, wrapped in each other's arms. There's no other way to put it: they were hugging.

I can't handle this level of cuteness!

Her mouth was agape in amazement. She watched the cats for a bit longer before returning to the living room.

"Hajime's cuddling with Shasha," she told her mother.

"Maybe Hajime feels a bit like a mother to her."

"Right." Reona felt her chest tighten at this observation from her mother. Apparently, grown cats, too, found the cuteness of kittens soothing.

And her mother also looked calmer than usual.

"Looking at Shasha brings back memories of when Hajime was little. Tomoya insisted we take her in, but it was tough because she was so small. She had just been introduced to solid food—she kept spitting it up, and her poop was all runny."

"Really?"

Reona had been five or six when Hajime joined their household. In her memories, Hajime hadn't seemed that small and hadn't required much care. To Reona, Hajime hadn't been so much a cute kitten as a playmate and peer.

"Tomoya was struggling to keep up with his school-work and was having trouble with his friends. It was a difficult time. I figured a cat might be a comfort to him, but ultimately, Hajime didn't really warm up to Tomoya. Even so, Tomoya's such a kind soul—he did his best to take care of her."

"Hajime bonded with you, though, didn't she?"

"Yes. It must've been tough for Tomoya to see."

There was a distant look in her mother's eyes. All thoughts, apparently, led to her brother. Reona smiled, amused by her mother's inability to wean herself off her son.

"But Tomoya has his own cat now," said Reona. "He hasn't brought him over even once. I'm sure Hajime would get along with his cat. Maybe we'll arrange a play-date sometime."

"Tomoya's cat is black. You don't like black cats, right?"

What is she talking about? Before Reona could ask, she heard a noise from the foyer. Her father was back from work. He came home late every night, looking exhausted.

"Oh, man, I'm beat. I'm not that hungry, so I'll have something simple for dinner. How are the cats? Did they fight?"

"There's some salmon, rice, and tea, so I can make some ochazuke. The cats are asleep in the back room. They're getting along nicely."

"Excellent," said her father, but Reona knew he didn't care enough to check on them. Instead, he turned to her. "How about you? How are you doing?"

"Good."

"How's school?"

"It's okay."

"I see."

It was a brief exchange, but since Shasha had joined them, there had been a slight increase in their conversations. It felt like one more member had been added to their family.

———

"Maybe my mother feels guilty for having 'taken' Hajime away from my brother."

It was Saturday, eight days after the clinic prescribed Shasha to Reona. With no school, she had spent the morning relaxing at home before heading over to Shousuke's in the afternoon. She had brought Shasha with her in a pet carrier.

Shousuke lay Shasha on her back and scratched her tummy.

"So Hajime's your family cat? Originally, it was Tomoya who took her in, wasn't it?"

"Yeah. He had all sorts of pets growing up—bugs, fish, and stuff—but Hajime was the first big animal. I think he was disappointed when Hajime became attached to our mother instead of him. I mean, I'd be upset if Shasha bonded with only my mom. That's why I try to care for her as much as possible. I've even taken this week off from work."

Shasha was excited to have her stomach rubbed, and she nipped periodically at Shousuke's fingers.

"Ouch! This one's teeth are getting pretty sharp. The instruction leaflet said she should learn from play-fighting with her siblings, but she doesn't have any."

"Hajime is teaching her. Shasha tumbles around on her own, but occasionally, Hajime intervenes to stop her as if to say, 'That's enough!' Rather than playing with her, it feels more like Hajime is supervising her."

"But she still bites a lot. Maybe because of the big age gap, Hajime goes easy on her."

"Exactly. Something like that."

Hajime was a senior cat. It must be exhausting for her to keep up with the energetic Shasha.

"Ouch!" Shousuke drew back his hand. "Enough. That hurts. Reona, it's your turn."

"I don't want to be bitten either!"

"You have a cat, so you're used to this."

"Hajime doesn't bite or scratch. If something bothers her, she just hisses. It's my brother who's used to pain. You know he cares for the cats at the rescue center, and it's intense. His arms are covered in scratches, and he's even been bitten on the tip of his nose!"

"Taking care of rescues seems tough, with the cats acting out and trying to escape."

"Yeah. The amazing thing about Tomoya is that despite working so hard with cats all day, he also has his own at home. A few years ago, he adopted one of his rescues. At the time, I thought it was an unusual decision, but maybe the cat was a kind of replacement for Hajime."

"Because Hajime had become your mom's cat?"

"More or less." Reona lumbered toward the bed, eyeing Shasha. "To me, Hajime is like a family member, not a cat. So it doesn't bother me who she's closest to as long as she's healthy. But when Shasha came along, and since she's so cute, I started to feel like I wanted her to like me best. I guess it's a kind of possessiveness. If this was what it was like for my brother, I'm sure he had complicated feelings about it. And Tomoya is too kind to blame anyone."

"You've become softer toward your mom and brother, Reona. Maybe it's because you're taking two cats at the moment," said Shousuke.

Reona let out a strained laugh. *Does he actually think I've become more optimistic thanks to that weird doctor?*

Shousuke looked solemn. "In any event, I think you should avoid saying it."

"Saying what?"

"What you said at the clinic. That you hate your mom."

"Oh," she said. "I didn't mean that."

"There are some things people won't understand unless you say them out loud, but there are some things that, once said, you can't take back. It's best to keep harsh, irreversible things to yourself rather than expressing them emotionally."

"Shousuke, that was—"

"If you feel like you need to tell her, I'll be there with you. It really helped to have you there when I told my parents I was giving up on Kyoto University the other day. Things have been tense with my parents, and if you hadn't been there, I probably would've said something I'd regret."

"Really?"

"Yeah."

Shousuke was always cheerful and kind. Even someone like him had issues with his parents. It was somewhat comforting to know it wasn't just her.

"Thank you. But I really don't have anything I want to tell her. What I wanted to say . . ."

There are probably things I want to say. She realized this now. You couldn't see into a home from the outside. Once you stepped inside, you realized that each family inhabited its own world.

"No, there were things I wanted to say, but I already said them. So I'm okay."

Yes, that weird doctor allowed me to say what I wanted to say in his examination room.

It felt like something had come undone then.

She put Shasha back in the carrier and went home. As soon as she got in, her mother was there to greet her.

"Reona, Hajime has been searching for Shasha."

"Oh, really?"

She set the carrier down in the living room and immediately heard a meow. It was Hajime, approaching with her tail raised high. She appeared thrilled to have been reunited with Shasha, finally. Shasha also emerged from the carrier, her tail fluffy and upright like a hand-held duster. Both tails clearly conveyed their owners' feelings.

Reona watched. It was cute and heartwarming not only to see them so affectionate with each other, but also because her mother, too, was watching.

"Hajime really dotes on Shasha. She'll really miss her when she's gone."

"Yeah, she seems to want a friend."

"Well, there's nothing we can do—Shasha comes from Tomoya's rescue center," Reona said.

She felt a slight pang in her heart. By bringing Shasha home, she may have introduced Hajime to the feeling of loneliness, which, in turn, caused her mother pain. *I'll just adopt Shasha.* The thought had crossed her mind many times.

But the relationship with a cat was a long one. When Hajime first arrived at their home, Reona had still been a child. Now, she was an adult. Depending on their choices, she and Shasha might share a significant portion of their lives together. It was a major decision.

Her phone rang. It was from the yudofu restaurant. Today was her day off, and she had a bad feeling about it.

As she had expected, a coworker had called in sick, and the restaurant urgently needed her to fill in. She tried to refuse, but they begged her to come in. She hung up, feeling dismayed.

"Who was it?" asked her mother.

"Work. It seems they really need help, so I'm going in."

"If they need help, you'll just have to go in. I'll give Shasha her food, then."

Her face beamed. Shasha, hearing the mention of food, stepped toward her mother's feet. Reona was not amused.

Huh! she thought but then paused. Was she unamused because she felt Shasha had been taken from her, or was she simply jealous over her mother's attention toward the cat?

"I'm acting like a child!"

"Did you say something?"

"No, it's nothing. Thank you for taking care of feeding Shasha. Also, please make sure you give Hajime small portions and remove anything she doesn't finish. Tomoya said we should do that routinely."

"Really? Well, if Tomoya says so."

Just the mention of her brother put her mother in a better mood. She, too, acted like a child.

———

It was clearly a mistake to come in to help.

When she arrived at the restaurant, it quickly became apparent that it was beyond a matter of someone taking the day off and being short-staffed. Aside from the large-group reservations, a steady stream of customers kept the place constantly full. It was dizzyingly busy.

The waitstaff and kitchen crew worked nonstop until the final customer, after complimenting the delicious tofu, departed. When Reona went to the bathroom, she ran into her fellow part-timer who'd been working shifts all week. She, too, looked worn-out.

"Thank god you came in on your day off, Reona! It's actually my first time getting to use the bathroom today."

"Wow. You've been on shift all day, right?"

Reona, too, had not been to the bathroom since arriving, but she hadn't felt the need to go. She had been so busy that she hadn't had time to drink water.

"I was so busy that I didn't have time to take a break," said her colleague. "In the past, I've gotten a UTI from holding it in for too long. Have you ever had a UTI before?"

"No, I haven't. You need to take care of yourself."

"I will. I'll do the rest now, so you go home. A little kitten is waiting for you. Every moment of kittenhood is precious."

Cat lovers are so generous when it comes to felines, thought Reona.

Reona thanked her profusely. Her legs felt wobbly, and a creeping drowsiness made her body feel warm. The cats were likely to be sound asleep, curled up together.

It was already ten o'clock when she got home. Perhaps because it was the first time in a week that she had been in to work, she felt extra tired. Her vision was blurry, and her body felt heavy.

Is something wrong?

She had initially thought it was just regular fatigue, but something definitely felt off. She felt feverish, and even though she had used the bathroom at the train station, she needed to go again.

She emerged from the bathroom, her back bent from the stinging pain. Her mother sat in her pajamas, watching TV.

"M-Mom."

Her voice sounded feeble even to herself.

Her mother furrowed her brow.

"What's wrong? You don't look well."

"There's a lot of blood. My urine was bright red."

"What?!" She placed a hand on Reona's forehead. "Oh no, you have a high fever. It's likely a UTI."

"R-really?"

Reona couldn't sit still due to the persistent stinging and itching in her lower abdomen.

"Let's go to urgent care right away."

Her mother dragged Reona's father out of the bath and made him get the car while he was still soaking wet.

The diagnosis was pyelonephritis, a medical condition she had never heard of. It indicated that the bacteria had multiplied and were causing inflammation in her kidneys. The doctor informed her that the causes were not going to the bathroom for an extended period and dehydration.

Reona was admitted for the night. She lay on her back in bed while receiving antibiotics intravenously. Her mother sat beside her in a folding chair.

"You're really something else. Cats are prone to kidney problems, and here you are, the owner, getting sick instead. What are we going to do with you?"

"Sorry. I should've drunk more water. It was so busy, it slipped my mind."

She couldn't believe that dehydration had landed her in the hospital.

She stared up at the ceiling. Since she had never been seriously ill, hospitals unsettled her. The air was dry; the sheets were cool. She was anxious.

But her mother was by her side. She would always be there for her. At that moment, Reona even wished her mother could sleep next to her, as she had when she was little. Of course, she knew that wasn't possible now, but she realized that anxiety and loneliness brought on this feeling. This must be why the two cats at home hugged each other tightly in their sleep.

"Were Hajime and Shasha cuddling in their sleep again today?" Reona uttered her question toward the hospital room ceiling.

"They may have woken up from the commotion, but they'll fall asleep soon enough. Especially the kitten; they really do sleep all the time anyway."

"When Shasha leaves, Hajime will be all alone again."

"It is what it is. Tomoya's cat has always been alone, hasn't he? That's just the way it goes."

It's Tomoya this and that again. Laughter bubbled up inside Reona.

"Tomoya's cat . . . We really should ask Tomoya to bring him over one day. He said he's very gentle."

"What are you talking about? You don't like black cats, remember?" Reona's mother scoffed in disbelief.

Not again. She had said that before. Reona continued lying on her back and tilted her head.

"I don't dislike black cats. I like all cats."

"You say that, but when Tomoya brought home his first cat, you were terrified because it was black and made a huge fuss. Don't you remember?"

Reona's mouth fell open.

I was scared of black cats? Tomoya's first cat?

Her mother was laughing.

"You just kept crying and crying because some black cat in a manga used evil magic. You were so upset that Tomoya had no choice but to return the kitten to his friend. He thought it would be distressing for both you and the cat if it stayed. He's always so kind and caring toward you. So, in place of the black cat, we got Hajime, who also needed a home. You really don't remember any of this?"

"No . . ."

No matter how hard she traced her memory, she couldn't recall the black kitten. It had been returned to its original home because she had rejected it. And Hajime, who joined them instead, had pretty much rejected Tomoya.

That doctor had said, "There's no way of knowing if your choice might end up changing something for someone."

Reona's actions had impacted many people, but it was unclear if the outcomes were good or bad. Was it a good thing that Hajime came to their home? What had happened to the cat that was returned?

What if the black cat had become part of their family? Her brother would surely have adored it. He doted on Hajime, too, but he would have likely cherished it even more. If that had been the case, would he have taken his current job? Had it influenced him in some way? Tomoya had later adopted a black rescue cat. Was that cat a stand-in for the black kitten he couldn't keep due to Reona?

There was simply no way to know.

The next morning on Reona's return home, Hajime emerged to greet her. When they first got it, the chimes of the bell on her collar could be heard clearly from afar; now, it produced sounds as gentle as her movements.

Reona felt a soft head nuzzled against her instep, an interaction that had long since become routine for them.

"Hajime."

She dropped her gaze to the cat rolling about at her feet. As soon as she crouched down, Hajime darted away toward Shasha and lay down beside her. Reona had heard that cats with an age gap often had trouble getting along, so their friendship was not something to take for granted. Hajime was caring like her brother and had never once given her a scratch.

Suddenly, the words she really wanted to say came to mind.

"Hajime, thank you for joining our family."

She realized that not everything was a given. Her mother had brought Reona her things while she was hospitalized, and her father had taken time off from work to drive her mom to the hospital. None of these things could be taken for granted.

"Mom, Dad, thank you both so much."

"All right, all right. Make sure you take the full course of antibiotics they prescribed you. You mustn't stop taking them halfway."

Reona was startled at her mother's words. Today was the ninth day since she'd been prescribed Shasha. The doctor had said that if she was able to say what she wanted to say before the tenth day, she was welcome to return the cat early.

"I want to talk to you guys about something," said Reona.

Her serious face made her parents furrow their brows and exchange glances.

When she arrived at the clinic, she found the haughty nurse seated at the reception. "Ms. Kajiwara, you still have a day of the cat remaining, but you've come to return her already?" she said, without looking up.

"No, I left the cat at home. I have something I need to discuss with the doctor."

The nurse's eyes flicked up briefly to Reona. "I see. In that case, please head to the examination room."

As she waited nervously for the doctor, Reona wondered, *What should I do if he says no?* She suddenly felt regret bubble up. *I should've come earlier!* Perhaps they'd already arranged for someone to pick up Shasha.

The curtains in the back parted, and the doctor entered. Reona rose instantly from her seat and approached him.

"Excuse me!"

"Whoa! You startled me." The doctor shrank in surprise. "What's up?"

"What's up is that we want to adopt Shasha. We'll raise her lovingly as Hajime's little sister, so please let us adopt her. *Please!*" she begged, pressing the doctor against the wall. The doctor offered a wry smile.

"You're very, uh, intense. Our noses are almost touching. All right, all right. Have a seat. Take a deep breath."

Reona sat in the chair. She took a deep breath, then exhaled loudly.

The doctor smiled brightly. "How do you feel? Are you still upset with your mother?"

"N-no." Reona felt her face heat up. "It's fine now . . . I mean, I never really hated her. It was just that I was a little bit jealous that she always seemed to pay more attention to my brother."

The doctor burst into laughter. "A bit jealous? Ha-ha!"

"Ha-ha . . ."

She wished he wouldn't keep repeating what she'd said. Suppressing her embarrassment, she went on calmly. "I feel grateful for my parents—for all they do for me, including the things I normally take for granted. I also feel grateful for our cat, Hajime. Seeing Hajime happy made me appreciate Shasha, too. I'll take good care of them so they can both remain happy. I've already gotten my family's approval. Please let us have Shasha."

Please let Shasha still be available for adoption. May she be destined to be part of our family.

"Hmm . . ." The doctor sounded amused. Reona looked up and saw the doctor smirking. "I thought you'd come sooner. You took your time."

"I-I'm sorry. It took some courage to decide on having another cat."

"Well, it's a long-term relationship, so I guess you need time. But if only you'd come a little earlier, just a little earlier."

"Oh . . ."

Reona was aghast. The shock nearly brought tears to her eyes.

Suddenly, the curtains flew open with great force. The nurse marched in, glaring at the doctor.

"Dr. Nikké! Why are you being pointlessly mean?" she shouted. "Until a moment ago, you were uncertainly contemplating whether you should extend the prescription." She then put on a somewhat calmer expression and turned to Reona. "The kitten is from a reputable breeder. If you're interested in taking her in, I'll give you their contact information so you can handle the arrangements yourself. But I'll be honest: it'll cost you. That's just how it is with breeders."

"O-okay."

Reona quivered under the nurse's penetrating glare, but she nodded deeply.

"I have money saved up from my part-time job, so I should be all set."

"I see. Then, Dr. Nikké, no more nonsense from you. We're expecting the patient with an appointment soon," she snapped, and disappeared behind the curtains.

The doctor mumbled, "I mean, did she have to get super mad? I was just kidding . . ."

"Excuse me, doctor."

"Yes?"

"Is your name 'Nikké'?"

"It is. I used to have a different name, though. By the way, the breeder named the kitten 'Shasha,' but feel free to give her any name you like since she's becoming a member of your family."

Some cute cat names popped into Reona's mind, but they all disappeared. The spoiled one with a playful bite: Shasha. The one who was always napping: Shasha. Hajime's beloved companion: Shasha.

"I'm going to keep the name. Shasha's been Shasha from the start."

"I see," said the doctor with a smile.

It struck her anew that the doctor and her brother were like two peas in a pod.

When she left the examination room, the nurse called her to the reception and handed her a piece of paper with the breeder's information. Reona examined it closely.

"Excuse me."

"Yes?"

"Is the breeder someone I can easily reach? They're not like this place, are they? Hard to find depending on the day?"

"I have no idea," the nurse answered curtly. "I doubt it, but if you're concerned, why not ask your brother, the very knowledgeable, super reliable cat expert, to accompany you?"

Despite seeming uninterested in Reona, the nurse had remembered her snide remark quite well. Although the nurse was crabby, she had graciously shared the breeder's information with her. Like the doctor, she was quite odd. For some reason, Reona found this endearing.

"Actually, I was just putting on airs. My brother really is a cat expert, but it's an exaggeration to say he's super reliable. In fact, he can be absent-minded some-times."

"Oh?" The nurse's gaze flickered up to Reona. "But he's older than you, right?"

"At a certain age, sibling roles reverse, don't you think? In my family, it's my older brother people tend to worry about."

"Really? Is that so? Well, it's none of my business. Now, take care." Her expression turned blank again.

When Reona emerged onto the street, she glanced back down the alley. It was dimly lit, and hard to see what lay at the end. From today, she was the owner of two cats. It was unlikely she'd return here to be prescribed another one.

But if she met anyone with a problem, she would consider suggesting a visit to Dr. Nikké and his Nakagyō Kokoro Clinic for the Soul.

Nikké

4

Nikké

When had he begun to dread going home? Tomoya Kajiwara paused for a moment, his hand still gripping the doorknob of his front door. He held his breath and strained his ears. The only sound he could hear was the soft buzzing of the fluorescent lights in the hallway.

He let out a small sigh and entered his apartment. It was pitch-black. He switched on the lights, set down his bags, and shook off his jacket. He avoided looking around until he had completed this routine. This was what his everyday looked like. No dropping work to rush home, no bursting into his apartment in a panic. Once he completed his tasks, he finally turned his gaze to the three-tiered cat pen. It was a stainless steel enclosure, almost as tall as Tomoya. There were alternating shelves, and at the very top hung a hammock.

A hammock that was no longer in use.

At the lower level, a black cat lay curled up, tucked between the litter box and the water bowl. His face, turned toward the wall, remained hidden. His shiny black fur rippled softly from his rear to his back. Tomoya watched him breathe for a moment.

"Nikké."

Tomoya sat in front of the pen with one knee raised. The black cat remained asleep, showing no movement. After observing for a while longer, he opened the pen's door and checked the food and water bowls. About half the food was left, and the water was about a cup lower than it had been that morning. He pulled out the litter box to check the waste and was relieved to find that the minimum requirement had been met once again today.

"Nikké, shall I brush you?"

He gently lifted the black cat with both hands, making sure to support his feeble, dangling limbs so his head wouldn't loll around. Using his knee to help with positioning, he carefully pulled Nikké out of the pen. Then he nestled the cat comfortably on his back between his crossed legs, leaving his belly exposed. With a rubber cat brush, he carefully started to brush his fur.

"See, doesn't that feel good?"

He lifted the cat's forelegs and made gentle brush-strokes against his flank. Grooming was easy because the cat neither resisted nor showed any signs of discomfort, but instead, he had to be careful not to overdo it. Eventually, he stopped.

I wish he'd resist a bit.

The whiskers above his eyes and on his cheeks were black. His nose was also black, and even his paw pads were black. Unless you looked closely, it was hard to distinguish his features when he was asleep. He looked like he had been carved out from midnight, with his full-moon-colored eyes. When he strode elegantly under the fluorescent light, his black fur used to gleam. But it had been a few months since Tomoya had seen the cat do anything like that. In fact, he hadn't even glimpsed his cat's golden eyes in a long time.

"There you go, Nikké. You're all groomed. Now, sleep tight."

He gave the cat one last squeeze and buried his face in the back of his neck. The cat smelled wonderful—like freshly laundered bedding hanging in the sun. He cupped Nikké's head in his palm, ensuring it didn't hang too low. The sleeping cat's breathing was soft and steady, his freshly brushed body velvety and relaxed. As always, only his tail remained rigid, gently swaying even now. Tomoya liked to think Nikké was having a pleasant dream. He laid Nikké down in the enclosure, gently traced his back with his fingers, and closed the door.

Tonight, Nikké did not awaken either.

— · —

"Something bothering you, Kajiwara?" asked Mr. Ōta, the director of the rescue center.

Tomoya was hosing down litter boxes in the back of the facility. As usual, he wore rubber boots and gloves.

"A lot," replied Tomoya. "Figuring out how to stabilize operations. Getting our part-timers to stick around."

He smiled thinly and began scrubbing the donated crates and food bowls. Even if items were donated in pristine condition, they had to be given a thorough cleaning before being brought into the facility. Animals could carry all sorts of illnesses, and it was essential to protect the cats at the facility from infectious diseases.

He had a mountain of tasks to complete. He could

clean all day and still not be caught up. Tomoya's responsibilities were wide-ranging and included administrative work as well as field visits. Naturally, his worries were endless.

Tomoya had started working at the City Cat Rescue Center about seven years ago. Although he held the fancy title of "deputy director," his responsibilities included washing and cleaning up after the animals. They were often short-staffed, so full-time employees and part-time workers shared equal duties.

Mr. Ōta was a good-humored man in his late fifties. He, too, despite being the director, was often called upon to prune the shrubs and change light bulbs. Even now, he was dressed in coveralls and held a garden sickle in his hand.

"I'm not talking about work matters but, rather, personal issues. You know you can talk to me if something's troubling you in your private life."

"Why do you ask? Do I seem troubled?" Tomoya gave a strained smile while he hosed down a basket.

"That's not what I mean. It's just that recently, you seem . . . exhausted."

Ōta's tone was hesitant. Tomoya knew that normally, his boss didn't have time for idle chatter, but he had come all the way to the back of the building to speak with him. He knew that he wasn't here on a whim.

Tomoya removed his rubber gloves and used a small brush to scrub the stubborn dirt from the corner of the basket.

"We're both equally tired with how busy things are every day. There's probably more weighing on your mind than mine, Mr. Ōta. We don't want the next adoption fair to go like the last one."

"Ugh, yes, that left a bad taste," said Mr. Ōta. "We definitely need to have a team meeting before the next one."

Tomoya had succeeded in distracting him.

He turned off the faucet. His shirt was soaking wet. The weather was nice, so he left the freshly washed items to dry in the sun.

He was about to head out in his truck to pick up supplies and reported lost cats. When he got back, it would be time for grooming. While the gentler cats could be handled by other staff, the more aggressive ones required several attendants to handle. It was usually Tomoya who ended up covered in scratches.

"Mr. Ōta, I'm heading out to pick up three cats from

animal control. If we want to meet about the event, can we do that after I get back?"

"Yes, of course. That's a lot of cats we're picking up. The pet cat population has been increasing, but so has the number of cats arriving at our rescue center—I wish more people knew about this. Managing this operation has been a continuous struggle." Mr. Ōta sighed deeply, then shook his head vigorously. "No, no. Dark moods are strictly prohibited. This center's motto is 'Pawsitively bright and purrfectly clean.' Come on, Kajiwara, say it with me. 'Pawsitively bright and purrfectly clean!'"

"I'll pass," replied Tomoya before leaving Mr. Ōta on his own. He was a good man, but sometimes Tomoya couldn't keep up with his boss's high energy levels. Tomoya had never been comfortable with lively environments. Even if people labeled him dull or quiet, he preferred to do things at his own pace.

At the cat rescue center, challenges abounded, including harrowing situations that were difficult to face directly. But even then, Tomoya never looked away or let his composure falter, handling everything calmly. Personal emotions could hinder ongoing rescue efforts—he could cry or grieve after completing the tasks at hand.

Numerous workers, both full-time and part-time, had unfortunately left the job, unable to cope with the emotional toll.

That was why Tomoya operated at his own rhythm. This approach allowed him to manage his emotions and systematically complete his tasks. Until now, this method had been effective for him.

—·—

"Is something on your mind?" asked Madoka Terada, who sat in the passenger seat.

Tomoya kept his expression neutral as he held the steering wheel.

"You're making a big deal out of nothing. It was just a minor screwup," he said, avoiding her eyes.

"That's exactly what worries me. You don't usually 'screw up.' And it's been happening more and more recently." Madoka's tone was light but contained concern.

Tomoya pretended not to notice it.

"What else have I messed up?"

He knew he was feigning ignorance. Today's mistake was glaring. They had driven to collect the supplies, only to discover that no order had been placed. This mistake was his own. The items he thought he'd ordered—cat food, litter, and pee pads—were all running low. Thankfully, the vendor took pity on them, letting Tomoya take the supplies and place the order after the fact, even throwing in some discounts and special offers for the rescue center. Tomoya could do nothing but apologize.

He also had an idea of the other mistakes Madoka was referring to. He was mixing up dates and times because he kept zoning out. He couldn't afford to be so absent-minded. When he was, negative feelings arose, and he inevitably missed his appointment. Even when he tried to stay focused, his mind still wandered to something else in the back of his thoughts.

"Even yesterday, you forgot we had a meeting. If you forget, who's going to remind me?"

"We were both late for that one."

Tomoya laughed at the memory. When he had rushed to Madoka's desk to call on her, he found her fast asleep at her desk, seemingly unaware that their break time had ended.

"Exactly! It's a problem. At home, I have my daughter to wake me up. At work, I have you. That's how I can nap in peace. Wait, what were we talking about? Oh, right. Is something on your mind?"

Madoka's conversations often veered off topic, but today she managed to correct course.

"If you're tired, you should really consider cutting back on your workload. You work the most overtime and handle all the out-of-town assignments yourself. You don't even take a day off every week, do you?"

"I've taken time off here and there. I went to my parents' place the other day and relaxed a bit." Tomoya laughed it off.

Madoka, a little older than Tomoya, was a single mother with a child in elementary school. She had been working at the center for almost as long as he had. Although she wasn't particularly fond of cats, she chose this job for its proximity to her home. Her child, who was still a baby when she had begun working, was now in fourth grade.

"Mr. Ōta is a little worried about you, too," Madoka said, her tone more serious than usual. "If you collapse or quit, everyone at the center will be screwed. When you talk to people at our adoption fairs, we somehow find adoptive families for our cats very easily. You must have a knack for spotting destined connections."

"That's merely coincidental. Our cats find homes because our trainers care for them daily, preparing them for adoption. In fact, I'm the least likely person to have any destined connections with cats." The last line was spoken offhandedly, yet it sent a chill down his spine.

Madoka didn't seem to notice.

"Anyway, if you have something on your mind, you shouldn't keep it to yourself. You should talk to someone. I heard about this from my daughter—apparently, there's an excellent mental health clinic near Dr. Kokoro's practice."

"Dr. Kokoro Suda's practice?"

"Exactly. My daughter's classmate's parent's acquaintance's child apparently goes to that clinic. You turn either right or left on Rokkaku Street."

"That's extremely ambiguous."

"Addresses in that area are super confusing—north of this and south of that. When I first moved to Kyoto after getting married, I thought they made the addresses perplexing on purpose, and it really bothered me. My ex, who was all proud of his 'ancient capital of Japan' roots, was all about using those old-fashioned addresses. Turns out that his family was from Yamashina, which is basically Shiga Prefecture! But when I pointed it out to him, he blew up and was all, 'Yamashina's technically within the city of Kyoto.' Honestly, they say a relationship between a Tokyo woman and a Kyoto man never works out . . . Oh, I've gotten off track again. I'll send you the clinic's address later. Dr. Kokoro sees your cat, doesn't he? Why don't you drop by the clinic the next time you have a vet appointment?"

Dr. Kokoro Suda, the veterinarian at Suda Animal Hospital on Tominokoji Street in Nakagyō Ward, worked part-time at the cat rescue center. A compassionate man, he performed exams at the center and even made house calls when necessary. He had been the one to examine Nikké when he was rescued and did his best to save the other cats that were found at the same time. Sadly, only two cats survived the horrific abandonment. That had been three years ago.

Trying to sound as indifferent as possible, Tomoya replied, "My cat isn't being seen by Dr. Kokoro."

"Oh, really? Did you switch vets?"

"Yes, Dr. Kokoro's clinic is a little too far from my apartment."

"Oh, then you might not be in that area often, huh? Visiting a mental health clinic can be daunting, so I thought it might be good for you to go to one with a solid reputation. You know, sometimes just talking about your problem can make you feel better. I'd be willing to listen to your problems, but according to my daughter, when she talks with me, the conversation tends to jump around, and that leaves her feeling even more confused."

A faint chuckle escaped Tomoya. He continued to smile as he kept his gaze fixed ahead.

"Thanks for worrying about me. If I'm ever in the area, I'll be sure to drop by the clinic."

"Good. Good. You do that."

Madoka looked relieved. Both Mr. Ōta and Madoka were good people—they were kind to cats and people. They didn't know that Tomoya was a terrible person, unworthy of their benevolence. He felt guilty that they were worried about him. If he let out the emotions he'd bottled up inside, he'd cause trouble for everyone.

That's why he couldn't speak to anyone at the rescue center. He didn't want to discuss it with his friends or family. He hated the idea of even putting it into words.

There were some things that should remain unsaid.

Even so, he wondered if saying it out loud might bring some relief. Thoughts of the mental health clinic lingered in his mind.

— · —

An opportunity to visit Dr. Suda quickly arose.

Located on a narrow street in Nakagyō Ward, Suda Animal Hospital was sandwiched between wooden town houses, with the rear of the building serving as a residence. A long-standing establishment, it lacked modern medical equipment, and the X-ray and blood-testing devices were outdated. Examinations tended to rely on palpations and the vet's judgment based on his experience.

He primarily worked with dogs and cats. While veterinarians might not be familiar with every animal species, pet owners often assumed that vets could treat all kinds. As Tomoya looked at the patient photos displayed in the waiting room, he developed a deep appreciation for the complexities of a veterinarian's role. One image featured a small turtle about the size of a palm. To its owner, the turtle was a cherished family member. They likely sought help at this vet due to some issue.

I wonder if the turtle fully recovered. I hope it went on to live a long life.

The door to the examination room opened, and Dr.

Suda stepped out. He took off his surgical cap and mask, revealing a shock of white hair and a warm smile.

"You made the right decision, Tomoya."

Tomoya breathed a sigh of relief at Dr. Suda's gentle voice.

"Thank goodness. How many kittens did she give birth to?"

"Two big ones."

Dr. Suda looked toward the operating table. The mother cat was already curled up in a ball in a crate. Under her belly, newly born kittens with damp fur squirmed feebly.

"The mother cat is still young, and I believe she's a mix of slender foreign breeds. Siamese cats, for example, often have difficult births. It's fortunate you noticed. I wouldn't expect any less from you."

Dr. Suda cleaned up after the emergency cesarean section and removed his surgical suit. Cats usually managed birth on their own, but this one had been in obvious distress when Tomoya picked her up from the police station. He'd gotten her into the crate in the back of his van and was driving for a while when he realized something was seriously wrong. He knew at once the labor was taking too long. He'd seen enough normal births to know this was different. He was worried she wouldn't even make it back to the center. That was when he thought of Suda Animal Hospital.

When he rushed into the hospital, the morning appointments had already been completed, and the receptionist had already left. If Dr. Suda hadn't been in his residence in the back, Tomoya would have had to drive the suffering cat around in his back seat to another emergency vet.

"I am genuinely grateful for you. When I noticed the cat was going into labor in the back of the van, I broke out in a cold sweat."

"Did you go to the police station specifically for this cat?"

"I was out running another errand when the police contacted me about a cat they had rescued, mentioning that she seemed weak and needed to be picked up. So I took a detour to fetch her. I'm glad I did. It could have been dangerous if we had left her alone. I'm grateful to the officer who reached out to me."

"I see," said Dr. Suda with a nod.

"I apologize for making you see her during your

break. Since she hasn't yet gone through intake at the center, I'll pay for her medical bills separately."

"I forgot to do the intake paperwork for her myself. I'll charge you at cost. You should leave her here at the hospital tonight. I'm going over to the center on Sunday, so I'll bring her along then."

"Thank you for all that you do for us always."

Tomoya bowed. Veterinary treatments were costly. There was no public health coverage for animals, so one had to pay all expenses. Fees varied widely among vets, but higher costs didn't always guarantee better treatment. Still, as someone closely involved with the center's operations, Tomoya was painfully aware of the significant expenses required for facility maintenance and staffing.

Animals cost money—there was no sugarcoating this fact.

"How's your cat doing?"

Tomoya was taken aback. Dr. Suda was, as always, very gentle. He didn't mean anything by the question, but Tomoya's guilty conscience caused him to break out in a sweat.

"Same as usual. He's always asleep and seems to move around only when I'm not there."

"Is that so? Well, as long as he's active, that's good. If you're curious about his movements, you might consider installing a pet monitor."

"A pet monitor . . ."

I can watch Nikké during the day from work?

For a moment, he recalled Nikké's stretches: front paws to the floor, butt high in the air, back bowing in a long, satisfying arc. It had looked so relaxing that Tomoya had felt like trying it himself.

But he had not seen such a gesture in a long time.

The pet monitor was a good idea, but if he could, he'd watch Nikké constantly. He'd be checking on Nikké not only on his break but also during work hours. He imagined how restless he'd be and smiled wryly.

"No, even if I set up a monitor, I won't have time to check on it."

"I see. Well, if anything comes up, feel free to let me know. Don't keep it all to yourself."

Tomoya bowed. It struck him then that many people around him were concerned for him, and he felt a pang of embarrassment. His emotions must be just that obvious.

As he left the animal hospital, he considered how he

could develop that kind of inner strength. He admired Dr. Suda's ability to remain calm under any circumstance. The more Tomoya focused on work, the more a sudden, unsettling anxiety would overwhelm him, making him want to abandon everything. Sooner or later, he was going to make a significant mistake.

Should I speak to someone, even if it's just for temporary peace of mind?

If he wasn't wrong, the mental health clinic Madoka had texted him the address for was around here. "East of Takoyakushi Street, south of Tominokoji Street, west of Rokkaku Street, north of Fuyacho Street, Nakagyō Ward, Kyoto. Nakagyō Kokoro Clinic for the Soul. Fifth floor." Tomoya laughed at the chaotic address, but he thought it might be worth a visit.

As he walked down the street, Tomoya frowned. "*Huh?*" The rescue center's van, which he had parked near Suda Animal Hospital, was nowhere to be found. It seemed that, in a daze, he had walked in the opposite direction.

"I'm seriously ill."

He was alone on one of the grid-like streets of Nakagyō. One wrong turn, and he'd end up completely lost. He peered down the dark alley, thinking there couldn't possibly be a building back there. But there it was: an old, narrow structure at the far end.

"What in the world . . . ?"

He approached the building with wonder. It resembled the one from which Nikké was rescued, but that building had been on a main street and hadn't been as gloomy.

Strange. He recognized the hallway that extended from the always-open entrance of the building. Three years ago, holding his nose against the awful stench that permeated the place, he had the building manager let him into the unit. Inside, there were small cages stacked on top of one another, each containing a cat. He immediately understood what had happened.

Tomoya took the few cats that were barely breathing out of the cages and rushed them to Suda Animal Hospital. It was then that Nikké, despite being on the verge of death, had bitten him. He still had the scars on his arm.

He entered the building, feeling doubtful. On the fifth floor, he stood before the second unit from the back. This was where Nikké and the other cats had been abandoned.

When he touched the doorknob, it turned smoothly

with hardly any effort. The interior of the once-dark room had transformed entirely, and he felt his anxiety dissipate. It made sense; a new tenant must have moved in. There was a small reception window in the front. *Maybe this is the rumored clinic.*

The sound of slippers smacking on the floor resonated as a nurse appeared, a woman in her mid-twenties.

"Mr. Tomoya Kajiwara, we've been waiting for you."

"Oh?"

How does she know my name? The nurse gestured with her eyes toward the back of the room.

"The doctor is currently with a scheduled patient. Please have a seat and wait."

"That's okay. I'll come another day."

"Mr. Kajiwara, you have an appointment as well. Because it took you so long, others went ahead of you." The corners of the nurse's lips quirked up, but it was more of a smirk than a smile. There was a coquettishness about her that he found discomfiting.

But when he looked carefully, he found her face familiar. The nurse furrowed her brow as he stared.

"Is there something wrong?"

"Have we met before?"

"What is this? Are you hitting on me?"

"*What?*"

His face flushed scarlet, and he broke out in a cold sweat.

"N-no, I wasn't hitting on you. I just thought we might have met before."

Seeing beads of sweat appear on his forehead, the nurse snickered.

"That's an old pickup line. I won't fall for it. Please take a seat and wait. You can't leave. The doctor has been waiting for you all this time."

"O-okay."

He hurried into the waiting room—a small room with a single armchair—too embarrassed to protest. He took a seat and shrank into himself. He recalled the exchange that had just occurred, and his face burned at the memory: *Have we met before?*

Eventually, the flush in his face subsided. He surveyed the area: simple, clean walls and ceilings—everything neat and orderly. There was no trace of the horrific scene of garbage and animal waste.

He heard later from the animal control officer that they had been unable to find the unlicensed breeder. Based on the cats they discovered, it appeared they were not dealing with purebred cats but rather mixed breeds that were either bred from pedigree cats or visually appealing mixed breeds. It was unclear whether the business had encountered financial problems or some other trouble—the reason for the breeder's disappearance remained unknown.

Tomoya didn't question how it could have happened. Human excuses meant nothing to him. He had done everything he could at the time, yet he felt responsible for the cats that hadn't survived. If he had arrived a day earlier, perhaps he could have saved them. The guilt lingered to this day.

Tomoya remained absorbed in his thoughts when the door to the examination room swung open. A young man, barely more than a boy, stepped out. He was short and had a round face. When he spotted Tomoya on the sofa, his eyes widened in shock.

Why is he staring? Do I know him? Tomoya returned the stare, then realized he was looking at a woman, not a boy. A woman with short hair and a boyish look. She seemed around the same age as his little sister, Reona. Her eyes were steely, and her mouth was set in a firm line. She clutched a pet carrier to her chest; a white cat was visible through the plastic mesh. He saw a flash of light blue and yellow. It was an odd-eyed cat.

A cat at a medical consultation?

"Ms. Ao Torii, please come this way," the nurse called out, waving a pale hand.

Almost simultaneously, a voice called from inside the examination room: "Mr. Tomoya Kajiwara, please come in."

Tomoya looked away from the woman, who continued to look at him with a peculiar expression, and walked into the examination room. The room was sparsely furnished, containing only a desk, a computer, and a folding chair. At the desk sat a man in a white lab coat.

"I apologize for the wait. When it rains, it pours. But sometimes, it's really quiet." The doctor spoke in a cheerful, light manner; he appeared around thirty, about his own age, and with a similar physique.

"My last patient also took a while to arrive. I got tired of waiting and considered looking for her myself, but just as I was peering out of the window, a different patient turned up! Then I got scolded. And then I took a nap, thinking no one was coming, and ended up getting scolded yet again. But I'm relieved that neither of you forgot and eventually showed up."

The doctor was very talkative. He had delicate features and looked calm and approachable. Yet, his smile seemed flippant and insincere. *Is this what psychiatric clinics are like? If that woman I saw earlier is a patient, does it mean you could bring cats to these appointments? Maybe it's a thing . . . ?* Tomoya pondered uncertainly.

The doctor gave him a smile. "It's been a while, hasn't it, Mr. Kajiwara? What brings you in today?"

The examination started unexpectedly. Tomoya felt overwhelmed with thoughts.

"Well, uh . . . I've become increasingly absent-minded at work lately, and I've been making mistakes. The people around me are worried and suggested I talk to someone about it."

"I see." The doctor smiled. It wasn't the flippant smile from before but one that Tomoya thought he recognized. "We'll prescribe you a cat. When you're feeling weary, don't just bear it on your own—you should lean on a cat. Not a single positive thing can come from dealing with it all on your own. As for how to administer the cat, you can bury your face in it, pet it, whatever you like. Even so, you can't leave it to the cat to do as humans want. Well, then . . ." The doctor began typing on his keyboard with the look of a child up to mischief.

"Which cat? A double dose of a very effective cat might be good. It'll attack the ailment with double the power." The doctor burst into a fit of giggles.

Tomoya sat dumbfounded as he watched the doctor chuckle to himself.

What is he laughing about? I don't get it at all.

The doctor cleared his throat. "That's weird. The patient from the other day found that joke really funny. Oh, well, it's okay." The doctor spun around in his chair and called out toward the curtains. "Chitose! Please bring the cat!"

Tomoya wondered if he was addressing the nurse from earlier. He felt tense, still somewhat uncomfortable about being misinterpreted as flirting with her. However, no one came.

"Chitose?" the doctor repeated, but there was no answer and no indication that she might be coming.

"Huh? Did she really leave as soon as my scheduled patient got here? Wow, that's so typical of her. How heartless. Do you think that's heartless, Mr. Kajiwara?"

Tomoya wasn't sure how to answer the question. *The nurse disappeared during an examination?*

The doctor crossed his arms and shook his head. Tomoya felt unsure about how to react to such theatrics. *If the examination isn't progressing, should I leave?*

Then, the curtains suddenly whipped apart. The nurse stood with her eyes narrowed.

"Who are you calling heartless? If I were truly heartless, I'd have left you a long time ago!"

"It was a joke!" The doctor chortled. "I'm used to being told off by you at least once a day—it's practically routine now. Ha! Oh, wait. Where's the cat we're prescribing to Mr. Kajiwara?"

The nurse had nothing if not an angry expression on her face.

"We don't have any. You just prescribed the last cat."

"*Really?*" The doctor turned back to his computer. "That's strange. I thought there were plenty of cats available. Hmm. What about Tangerine?"

"She said tourist season is in full swing, and the cat café is busy, so she can't make it."

"What about Bibi?"

"He's trying to compete in cat shows again. He wants to stick to his diet and not eat out."

"Margot?"

"She's expecting and currently on maternity leave.

Kotetsu and Noelle have found forever homes. Tank is busy looking for his future wife: his schedule is packed with dates."

"Dates, huh? That's nice. Hmm, I never thought we'd run out of cats. What should we do?" The doctor crossed his arms.

Tomoya didn't fully understand what was going on, but it seemed like it was a good excuse to leave.

"Well, in that case, I can go home tonight and . . ."

"Mr. Kajiwara has already been prescribed a cat from this clinic," the nurse said firmly, looking down at them both. "You need to check these things properly, doctor. There's already a cat on standby at Mr. Kajiwara's home. Until he finishes his current cat prescription, we can't issue another."

"But, Chitose . . ." The doctor appeared flustered. ". . . That cat's not very effective anymore."

"What are you saying? There's no such thing as an ineffective cat!" The nurse's shrill voice echoed through the examination room.

Tomoya shrank back. *This woman's obstinacy is no joke.* The doctor pursed his lips petulantly.

"Well, if we're out of cats, it can't be helped. Mr. Kajiwara, please try taking the cat you already have at home for one night. If that doesn't work, please come back, and we'll prescribe you a different cat . . . right, Chitose?"

"I suppose so," said the nurse coolly. "But I'll bet the cat will suit you. In fact, no other cat will work. You need to do everything to keep that frivolous, good-for-nothing sourpuss around no matter what. You need to dig your claws in and cling on."

The sparkle in the nurse's gaze was intense. It wasn't just her gaze; her voice and facial expression also delivered a powerful punch. She was looking at Tomoya, yet it felt like she was exerting pressure on something else entirely.

"You will get better. Unlike me, your cat is by your side, fighting hard. I doubt you'll need to come back here again. That concludes your checkup. Right, doctor?"

The nurse's eyes suddenly lost their light. A subtle smile lingered, but the cold, distant air she had previously projected was gone, replaced by a striking fragility.

The doctor ignored the nurse's change of demeanor.

"Now, Mr. Kajiwara, please give my regards to that sophisticated, cool, and handsome cat of yours." He fell into another fit of giggles.

What is up with these two? In the end, Tomoya left

the clinic without receiving any treatment. Hovering outside the building, he looked up—it was indeed the place where he had found Nikké and the others.

He ambled out of the alley in confusion and immediately spotted his parked van. *My sense of direction is off.* He needed to get going. He was still on the clock but had spent quite a bit of time on a personal matter.

When he got back to the center, he kept himself busy to prevent any unsettling thoughts from creeping in. Apparently, Tomoya looked particularly grave as he worked—even a bit scary, according to Madoka.

—— · ——

It was already eleven o'clock at night when Tomoya got back to his apartment. He gave a deep sigh as he switched on the lights. He used to be greeted by the sight of homemade cardboard cat houses and paper bags, and even a planter of cat grass. Now, everything had been tidied up, and the floor was clear. He dropped his bag and jacket and sank down onto the floor.

He remained cross-legged against the wall, unable to move, but when the thought of food finally prompted him to look up, he found Nikké sitting upright, staring back at him with golden eyes.

Tomoya was momentarily paralyzed. Nikké—all black, except for his eyes. His round, full-moon-like eyes.

He rushed to the cat pen.

"Nikké! Nikké! Long time no see!"

In his haste, he fumbled with the cage door. Once it was open, Nikké arched his back upward before approaching Tomoya. Tomoya scooped him up in his arms.

"Hey! You're looking energetic! It's been months since I've seen you moving around like this, and you've been asleep all this time. Did you eat your food? You wouldn't wake up no matter what, and I thought maybe you weren't going to make it."

With one fluid motion, he stroked Nikké from head to tail. Nikké's fur shimmered, smooth like velvet. He quickly darted away from Tomoya and gave himself a vigorous full-body shake. A cloud of fur fluttered into the air as he started to explore the room.

He was moving around fine. He was walking. There was no sign of weakness or unsteadiness; his back and tail formed a strong, straight line. *Am I misremembering?* Nikké appeared younger than before, his face resolute and his fur shiny.

But none of that mattered. Tomoya was just ecstatic that Nikké was awake.

"Here, let me take your food and water bowls out."

He took them out of the cage and placed them in the room. Then he rummaged through his closet for some toys. When he turned around, Nikké had his head buried inside his work bag.

"Hey, that's off-limits."

However, Nikké took one, then two jumps into the bag and slowly lowered his rump. He glanced back at Tomoya with a twinkly look and remained still.

He did what he wanted. He didn't do what he didn't. Tomoya felt heat build behind his eyes as he observed Nikké's expressionless demeanor that showed no hint of shame nor flattery.

About a year ago, Nikké stopped waking up even when lifted or shaken. He wouldn't open his eyes during brushing or face wiping. However, he didn't appear comatose; he seemed to behave normally when Tomoya wasn't present. The amount of food and water in his bowls dwindled, and he continued using the litter box.

Tomoya brought Nikké to Suda Animal Hospital,

where both the X-rays and blood tests came back normal. Yet, even with his eyelids manually held open, he did not awaken. Dr. Suda diagnosed him with excessive sleeping caused by a decrease in physical capabilities. At the time Nikké was rescued, he was about one year old, and two years had passed since then.

It was too early for his body to be deteriorating.

But who knew if the poor breeding conditions had shaved off years from Nikké's natural lifespan. Tomoya took Nikké to Dr. Suda's a few more times, but witnessing Nikké's limp form endure injections left him feeling guilty and reluctant to return.

In the early days, before his "condition," Tomoya made sure to play with Nikké daily, regardless of how late he got home. Though "play" might be a bit of an exaggeration—it usually involved Tomoya watching Nikké play around on his own or, conversely, Nikké watching Tomoya work through some paperwork. They had a quiet sort of companionship.

Tomoya would even fall into a trance watching Nikké play. His coat was so shiny that the room's lights bounced off each strand of fur. Tomoya worked with dozens of cats at the rescue center, but the only cat that captured his heart was his own.

Their bond was stronger than he could have ever imagined. Back at his parents' house, there was Hajime, the family cat, but Tomoya secretly reveled in the fact that his connection with Nikké was uniquely his own— a notion so childish he kept it from his sister.

Even now, Nikké wasn't doing much, simply sitting like a statue in his bag, fixated on the spot where the wall and ceiling met. Perhaps there was something visible only to cats, but Tomoya didn't approach Nikké to see what had caught his attention. Instead, he observed his cat as he stared intently at that one spot.

I hope our hours of activity will overlap like this, just as they did before you got "ill."

He watched in silence until Nikké grew bored and climbed out of his bag.

⸺

Tomoya was wheeling a hand truck loaded with cat litter bags from the storage room to the cattery when Madoka came up behind him, also pushing a trolley.

"Did you end up going to the mental health clinic?" she asked.

"I did, but I left without receiving any treatment."

"Really? They didn't even listen to your problems?"

"They did, and they didn't."

"Wait. Which was it?"

"The doctor was really talkative, so it was more like I listened to *him*. But it was a fun experience and a nice change of pace."

"So, it was a good clinic. That's great to hear! You have me to thank," said Madoka.

She sounded happy. Tomoya kept his gaze forward and smiled. "That's true. Drinks are on me on our break today."

"Yay! But to be honest, I wanted to hear from someone who has actually been to the clinic. My friend's daughter is having a tough time and is looking for a good therapist."

"So I was a guinea pig." Tomoya laughed. It was very Madoka to be so candid.

"What was the doctor like? Were they kind?"

"The doctor was a young man—maybe around my age? He was kind of flippant, and the nurse was pushing him around a bit. In any case, I didn't receive any formal treatment, but maybe that's how mental health care goes."

"I bet it is. You seem more cheerful."

Tomoya responded with a light laugh.

The fact that he had a little less to worry about had

nothing to do with the doctor. He now had something to look forward to when he went home, and apparently, that showed in his face, even at work. He didn't know he was that transparent. Until a few days ago, he had been making everyone worried.

They returned together to the office for a meeting about the upcoming adoption fair. As always, the meeting commenced with discussions on the selection of participating cats, updates on adopted cats, and reports on their publicity and awareness campaigns. Just as they were finishing up, Mr. Ōta brought up the problem from the last fair.

"The cats we put up for adoption have undergone two months of medical care and behavioral training at our center. We only send out cats that we consider ready to become new family members. So you don't need to worry too much about the criticism we received last time. It's just that—"

"I have to admit, I was hurt when that child saw one of our cats and burst into tears," said Madoka, sounding dejected. She had been the one to handle the rowdy family.

The adoption fairs were held once a month on the

center's most spacious floor and were open to the public. The adoption process required a review of paperwork and a trial period lasting several days. To prevent the illegal reselling of cats, a deposit system was implemented for the trial. Post-adoption, there was a significant amount of contractual paperwork and reporting in.

Even so, due to the recent animal welfare boom, they received a vast number of applications. The boy, around four years old, and his parents, who visited the center last month, were a typical example of those caught up in the excitement of the trend.

"They didn't fully grasp the concept of a rescue center. They arrived out of impulsive curiosity," Madoka recalled, propping her chin on her hand as she thought back to that day.

Ōta nodded. "There's no harm in anyone coming to the fair just out of curiosity. If we set our standards too high and become unapproachable, it could result in our downfall. I actually prefer that people feel relaxed rather than overly cautious when they come."

"I don't disagree. People need to meet our cats for connections to be formed. But people who visit our center with anticipation often seem to have quite a shock. I think we've grown accustomed to things here and have lost sight of how jarring it can be. We've particularly underestimated how sensitive children can be."

"Yes, that child was crying so hard."

"Even the parents were distressed."

Madoka and Mr. Ōta sighed heavily. Both were kind and good-natured. Tomoya, on the other hand, felt more sympathy for the rejected cats.

On their way out, Tomoya had had the opportunity to speak directly with the family. The boy had told him he had wanted a cat for a long time and had done his research by watching videos and looking at books. When he finally got his greatest wish to see the cats, what he encountered were not purebred cats with beautiful fur like those in pet stores and cat cafés. Instead, the cats at the center bore scars and looked fierce and intimidating. There were no cats displaying cute, charming behaviors that could bring a smile to anyone's face.

The boy, clutching a children's illustrated cat encyclopedia, was in tears. Tomoya's chest tightened at the boy's guilelessness. The boy's parents had not meant any harm either. When they had decided to get a cat, they thought they would be doing a good deed by adopting a rescue. A lack of research and knowledge ultimately hurt a child who had come with such high hopes.

"Maybe it *is* a bad idea to allow people with no experience or families with small children to adopt," said a team member. Other team members nodded in agreement.

The center's adoption policy was a topic of ongoing debate. The City Cat Rescue Center's policies were more lenient compared to other facilities.

"What do you think, Kajiwara?" asked Mr. Ōta, looking for backup.

"If we raised the bar, we'd see a clear decrease in adoption applications."

"Exactly. That's what I mean."

"But even if we received fewer applications, the success rate of those adoptions might increase proportionally. Of course, overall numbers would be lower than they are currently."

Mr. Ōta and Madoka exchanged looks. "What do you mean?" they asked simultaneously.

"Ultimately, I think those who are truly serious about adopting are just a minority," said Tomoya. "This might sound harsh, but many of the casually curious come here and learn the hard realities, and they leave feeling disheartened. If that leads them down a different path, then so be it. They might come back here, find another place to adopt, or maybe give up on adoption altogether."

He recalled the boy who had cried when he saw the cats. He knew the names of all the cat breeds, the boy had told him through his tears.

What choices will he make when he becomes an adult? Tomoya had thought.

Tomoya suddenly noticed that everyone at the meeting was staring at him. Feeling a bit awkward, he lowered his gaze.

"Altering our adoption policies will affect awareness, event attendance, and donation amounts. There are significantly more individuals who have never owned pets than there are pet owners. To be candid, our broad policy aims not just at adoption but also at engaging those who have never had pets, motivating them to back our initiatives financially. Increased attendance at our events translates into more donations."

"Well said!" Mr. Ōta's eyes lit up.

"How about we highlight this point in our ad for the upcoming adoption fair? We can be honest and say, 'For those without experience in cat ownership, visiting our center may be a bit challenging. Still, we would love for you to come.' What do you think?"

"That's it. Honesty is the best policy. This center's motto is 'Pawsitively honest and purrfectly healthy.' Now, say it with me, Kajiwara. 'Pawsitively honest and purrfectly healthy!'"

"No, I'll pass. The workday is officially over. May I leave for the day?"

"Oh, yeah, of course. How unusual for you to leave the office this early."

Tomoya gave a thin smile and slipped out of the meeting. In the past few days, he hadn't been putting in much overtime. On his way out, he crouched by the empty boxes from the supplies he'd transported earlier. Madoka approached him.

"Thank you, Tomoya."

"For what?"

"For tying everything together nicely at the meeting. Everyone knows you're kind, so that's why they embraced your idea easily."

Tomoya laughed and looked away. "I'm not kind. I'm actually a bad person."

"*What?*"

"May I take this box?"

"Of course, but didn't you take one home yesterday, too?"

"I messed up the holes on that one, so he didn't like it."

With that, Tomoya chose a random box and rushed
back to his apartment.

———

"Nikké, I'm home!"

As the door opened, Nikké took a few steps toward
him. For the past five days, whenever Tomoya got home,
Nikké had been awake. The sight of his cat's eyes open—
after Tomoya had almost lost hope—overwhelmed him
with emotion. He had started to leave the pen door open,
allowing Nikké to wander freely. Tomoya didn't mind if
the apartment got messy.

"Okay, give me a second."

Putting off his own dinner preparations, Tomoya began building a cardboard house. The holes on the side of
the structure that he had built the previous day were
apparently too big. Nikké had shown little interest, and
with a blank expression that still exuded some dissatis-
faction, he refused to enter it.

I won't mess this up today. Using a utility knife, he
meticulously carved a hole in the box. It was smaller

than yesterday's, just large enough for Nikké to poke his head out.

"Perfect."

Tomoya was very satisfied with the end product. But when he looked for Nikké, he found him sitting inside yesterday's failed cardboard house. Sticking only his head out from the box, he narrowed his eyes.

"Hey! This one's turned out a lot nicer, Nikké. Use this one."

Not wanting the better-structured cardboard house he had made to go to waste, he eagerly stuck his hand through the hole, pressing his cheek to the floor to peer through the opening, and did other sorts of things to appeal to Nikké. But Nikké, with only his head visible, gazed intently at the spot where the ceiling and wall met.

"I get it. Today, you're feeling that other one more. I guess I understand."

Cats' behaviors were unpredictable. He wasn't remotely disappointed or surprised that the house he had delayed his dinner to build was going unused. Instead, the betrayal of his expectations brought a smile to his face.

Tomoya sat cross-legged and watched Nikké staring at the wall.

"Listen, Nikké. You're pretending not to look at the

new house, but I know you saw it. I can sense you making comments about it in your head."

Nikké ignored him. Didn't even flinch.

But he was absolutely listening. And observing. And secretly poking fun at Tomoya with his entire being. His owner amused him, as he continued to flail frantically without getting any reaction from him.

"You're a good boy, Nikké. You really are."

Tomoya couldn't stop himself from talking to Nikké, who now resembled a toy popping out of a jack-in-the-box. He truly was a good boy. There was nothing more to say.

Tomoya's phone sounded—it was a message from his mother, urging him to let her know when he'd be visiting next. He smiled wryly; he had just seen them last month. Even then, he hadn't intended to stop by. He had felt an unexpected urge to do the normal thing of visiting his parents and had squeezed it into his schedule.

He became so busy on the day he had initially planned to go that he ultimately had to delay his visit until the next day. His sister found Tomoya's behavior unusual and became suspicious.

Tomoya had wanted to do something out of the ordinary to occupy his time. Eager to stay busy, he had pushed himself to take on more work. Consequently, he became unusually distracted, avoided going home to his apartment. Yet now, he was dashing up the stairs of his building, his feet light with joy.

Before he knew it, Nikké had emerged from the cardboard box and was making his approach. He gently pawed at Tomoya's leg before climbing up. Despite the instability, he settled atop Tomoya's knee and closed his eyes. When Nikké shut his full-moon eyes, he transformed into darkness. Tomoya felt a chill run down his spine.

"No, Nikké, you can't go to sleep."

Tomoya shook his knee; Nikké instantly opened his eyes. Gracefully, he returned to his pen and curled up into a ball. His eyes remained open, as Tomoya had wished. His eyes, which seemed to gaze into a void, appeared emotionless.

But surely, Nikké was aware of the truth. He knew what Tomoya was thinking. People around him might call him kind, but in reality, he was selfish and cold. Nikké understood the real reason Tomoya hadn't wanted to return to his apartment until recently—he saw right through it all.

Even so, the tenderness of Nikké staying awake for him was almost enough to crush Tomoya's heart.

— · —

A cautionary note was posted on the website, and the adoption fair was to be held as scheduled.

Starting Saturday morning, it was all-hands-on-deck. Tables were set up in the largest room at the rescue center, and cats in enclosures were brought out one by one. Several booths were established, including one for paperwork and another for selling merchandise, and a small area was cleared for educational workshops.

Tomoya was moving one of the enclosures with a cat inside, readjusting a plate with a number on it. As a rule, cats were referred to by numbers, even if they already had names. If a numbered enclosure became available, a new cat would take its place. This practice was unpopular because it felt like they were treating the cats as objects, but it was intended to prevent employees from becoming too attached to the cats, as well as out of consideration for the future owners. They sent off the cats, advising the new family to choose a new name for their pet.

Once everything was set up, Tomoya took a short break. He crouched down to meet the gaze of one of the cats.

"Wighead, you've been here for a while now. Let's hope someone nice comes for you today."

In crate nine sat a male cat with black-and-white fur. He was called Wighead because his face was mostly white, but the fur from his brows to the back of his head was black. Even though the cats were assigned numbers, they all eventually received nicknames organically. Wighead had been at the rescue center for nearly two years. He had been taken home for trials several times, but unfortunately, none had resulted in a permanent adoption.

Madoka, who had finished her own tasks, came over to Tomoya's side.

"I finished setting up the booths for the cats who are not up for adoption. I placed a large caution sign on the board to prevent kids from wandering over like they did last time," she said.

Tomoya smiled. After the meeting, someone proposed that they exclude the cats not eligible for adoption at the fair. But the suggestion was not accepted.

"I was taken aback by your outright rejection of the idea to exclude those cats." Madoka chuckled teasingly, which made Tomoya's face redden.

"Was I too harsh?"

"Not at all. Once you explained that raising awareness

about the reality of the situation could help reduce the number of cats needing to be rescued, I reconsidered my stance and found myself agreeing. Concealing unpleasant truths does not address the problem at its core."

"But we're only showcasing a small selection of the cats. Those with serious issues won't be taken out of the cattery. That's also the reality."

"If I recall correctly, your cat's also a rescue, right?"

"Yes, that's right. I adopted him before he came to this center."

"Why was that?"

"After he received medical treatment at Dr. Suda's, he came directly home with me . . ."

"That's not what I meant. Why did you pick *that* cat?" asked Madoka, as blunt as ever. "You're so good with all the rescue cats here. I've always been so impressed by how you can be so warm and yet maintain a clear, professional boundary. Was there a special reason you adopted that one? Was it fate? Did you feel a spark?"

Tomoya blinked rapidly. He'd never thought about his reasons for adopting Nikké.

Their first meeting had been harrowing. He had found Nikké lying limply in a cramped cage, covered in feces and urine. Tomoya had thought he was dead. When he slowly pulled him out of the cage, Nikké suddenly bared his fangs and snapped. He sank his sharp canines into Tomoya's arm, and blood came pouring out.

"Rather than a spark, I felt like I'd been struck with a violent bolt of lightning."

"Huh?"

Chattering voices began to fill the air. The adoption fair had started. Families with children, young women, a man accompanying his elderly parents—the attendees were diverse. Some had eyes sparkling with anticipation, while others kept a cautious distance. There was even a couple who exchanged an awkward glance and left right away. The cats' photographs were posted on the website in advance, but most of the cats at the rescue were not accustomed to cameras and did not photograph well. Many people noted how the cats looked completely different in real life, which was why the center urged people to visit the cats in person.

The staff were all busy explaining things to visitors. Tomoya assisted a woman who asked to see Wighead. She seemed experienced with cats, but Wighead nervously flattened his ears against his head. Was it chemistry or timing? Deciding it was better for them not to get too close, Tomoya chose not to hand the cat to the woman. After much consideration, the woman left.

"That was too bad."

Tomoya smiled at Wighead resting in his arms. Wighead gave a yawn, as if to say, "Oh, well!"

In moments like these, a touch of firm persuasion could pave the way to success. Yet, there were instances where the reverse held true. It was all very complicated— cats and humans. The tiniest details could alter everything in a moment.

Madoka approached him, looking bewildered.

"*That* family from last month is here," she whispered.

"You mean the one with the kid who bawled when he saw the cats?"

The floor was packed with people. Tomoya craned his neck and spotted the family amid the crowd— a young couple with a son around kindergarten age.

"They brought the child again, even though he was so frightened last time."

It was ill-advised of them to bring their child again, regardless of how interested they were in adopting a cat.

The boy had cried so intensely that it was as if he were on fire, and his loud cries had made all the cats anxious, forcing them to pause the adoption fair.

"I'm going to have a little chat with them. Take Wighead for me."

Tomoya went over to the family, who saw him coming. Looking sheepish, they bowed in greeting.

"We're really sorry about last month. You're the deputy director of this rescue center, right?"

"Yes, I'm Tomoya Kajiwara. Hello." Tomoya turned to the boy with a smile. "Hi, sonny."

"Hello!" the boy replied enthusiastically. He held out a picture book to him. "Here!"

"What is it?"

The boy persistently nudged the book toward him. Tomoya gasped. "Did you study up on rescue cats?"

It was a children's book about animal welfare. The book featured cute illustrations and large, easy-to-read text depicting what it means for animals and humans to coexist, the roles of animal shelters, and stories about abandoned cats and stray dogs.

On their last visit, the boy had been carrying an illustrated cat encyclopedia. However, today's book focused not on the charm of cats but on the difficulties of living with them. At the thought of the boy reading this book, Tomoya's eyes welled with tears.

"Our boy insisted on returning here, no matter what we said," the mother said timidly. "He's very stubborn. Once his heart is set on something, he sticks to it. Would it be okay for us to see the cats? I've told him he has to behave today."

"Yes, of course."

Tomoya handed the book back to the boy and bowed slightly. He felt embarrassed about his earlier comments regarding their policies. At the rescue center, he had encountered cats in a variety of situations and, without noticing it, had grown confident in his ability to make sound decisions. However, he understood that what was needed from anyone looking to adopt was sincerity. Even if they couldn't adopt right away, he believed they would show kindness in different ways elsewhere.

Tomoya spent the rest of the day explaining and answering questions. At some point, he noticed the boy and his parents chatting with Madoka. She held Wighead in her arms.

Madoka knelt in front of the boy as Wighead and the boy came close. He was reaching out his arms, attempting to embrace the cat, but Wighead's size made it impossible for a small child to lift him. Madoka stepped in to give him a shove.

The cat dangled lazily in the boy's embrace, showing no signs of struggle. Even when the boy squeezed him affectionately, Wighead looked like he was saying, "Do whatever you like."

I see. They must be destined for each other.

As Tomoya observed the family go to fill out their trial paperwork with Wighead in tow, he sensed that connections were not something one could influence. As he was leaving, the boy came up to Tomoya once more.

"My cat wears a helmet, so I decided to name him 'Helmet.'"

Tomoya laughed. "That's a cool name."

"How about yours?"

"What?"

"Your cat. Don't you have one?"

"I do have one. His name is Nikké."

"What is he like? What kind of cat is he?"

The boy was very curious. It was uncertain whether he would become Wighead's owner, but Tomoya hoped his interest in rescue animals would continue to ripple outward.

"My cat is black. A very kind black cat."

As he verbalized it for the first time, Tomoya realized that Nikké really was a kind cat. As he waved at the boy, he glanced at his forearm, where the scar from Nikké's bite was still visible. Nikké had snapped at him, even though he could hardly move at the time. Tomoya had let go in surprise, and Nikké had hissed at the other staff members. Ultimately, they were able to save only one other, a female calico, but perhaps Nikké was trying to protect the group. Perhaps they were family.

The adoption fair came to a close, and many of the cats left with their families for their trial period. How many would successfully convert to adoptions? Even after adoptions, the owners were required to provide status reports for a few years. They kept an eye on the cat until it passed.

After packing up equipment and completing paperwork, it was late at night before Tomoya left. He felt drained, both mentally and physically. In a fog, he returned to his apartment and switched on the light. He was too tired to eat. As he considered postponing all his to-dos until tomorrow, his gaze casually drifted around the room. That was when he saw Nikké lying completely still on the lowest shelf of the cat pen.

Tomoya's breath caught in his throat.

Before he could move, his thoughts began spinning out of control.

He's dead. He's dead.

He rushed to the pen and reached inside. Nikké lay still, eyes closed. Tomoya wrapped his hands around the cat's torso, causing his head to droop to one side. Extracting him from the pen took some effort.

"Nikké. Nikké."

He was warm. Tomoya gently stroked the cat's glossy stomach with his finger and saw it rising and falling.

Tomoya released a shaky breath. But no matter how many times he called his name or shook him, Nikké remained asleep. He didn't know if Nikké was now in a true coma or if, like before, he had been active during the day.

The vet nearest to his apartment offered emergency services, but none of the vets had been able to determine why Nikké wouldn't wake up. All tests indicated that Nikké was in perfect health. If anyone could help them, it would be Dr. Kokoro Suda.

The trains were no longer running at this hour, so Tomoya called a taxi. Regardless of whether it was an emergency or not, he could rely on Dr. Suda to take it seriously. He wrapped Nikké in a blanket and placed him inside a pet carrier. He called Suda Animal Hospital as he was leaving. After a few rings, Dr. Suda picked up, and as he got into the cab, Tomoya explained the situation.

Not fully grasping his own actions or what was right or wrong, Tomoya rushed into the Suda Animal Hospital in Nakagyō Ward. It was the middle of the night.

The service door was open in anticipation of his arrival. Dr. Kokoro Suda was dressed in pajamas and a lab coat when Tomoya rushed into the examination room and laid Nikké on the metallic exam table.

"I'm so sorry, Dr. Kokoro, for coming at this hour."

"It's no problem at all. The same as before?"

"Yes. He won't wake up, no matter what I do. Yet for the past week, he's been showing signs of movement again. He was so full of energy this morning."

"All right. Let's take a look."

Dr. Suda examined the completely immobile Nikké from various angles. He lifted his eyelids, pried open his mouth, took X-rays, and conducted a thorough evaluation. Nikké remained limp and unresponsive the entire time.

"As expected, the cause is unclear."

Dr. Suda sighed, his expression dark. Tomoya knew this would be the case, and he, too, let out a deep sigh.

"I see."

"I'm so sorry."

"Don't be." Tomoya shook his head. "Please don't apologize. You're the only vet who has so thoroughly examined Nikké. I know we don't understand what's wrong with him, and there's nothing we can do, but I just can't stand by and do nothing. Maybe he'll wake up tomorrow morning. I can only hope . . ."

"Usually, if a cat doesn't wake up upon receiving a shot, it suggests that they're in a coma. Yet during the day, he's active, eats, drinks water, and eliminates waste. I've never heard of a condition like this. I don't know how to describe it . . . I can sense his willpower or something like that."

Dr. Suda laid Nikké on a blanket and stroked his gleaming black fur.

"This one has always had a strong will to live. He should have died at that breeder's place, but he survived against all odds. It's possible that he's hanging on by a thread and clinging to life."

Tomoya was startled by Dr. Suda's words. Someone else had said something similar.

He looked at Nikké. His fur shone beautifully under the examination room's lights. He recalled how he had not wanted to go back to his apartment where the sleeping Nikké awaited him.

"Dr. Kokoro?"

"Yes?"

"Nikké doesn't have much time left, does he?"

Dr. Suda spoke quietly. "Probably not."

"When . . . ?" With hollow eyes, Tomoya gazed at Nikké, his eyes falling on the gentle hump of his tiny stomach, glimmering in a dark sheen.

He had hesitated to put it in words until now. He felt ashamed even to think it.

But he couldn't keep this murky turmoil inside any longer.

"When will he die?"

"Tomoya."

"Please tell me, when will Nikké die? I can't take it anymore. Dr. Kokoro, I can't stand this any longer. Ever since Nikké stopped waking up, every day I've been unable to concentrate on anything, worried that I'd find Nikké dead when I got home. I've been distracted at work, constantly making mistakes. And whenever I think that maybe Nikké might die at this very moment, I suddenly have to run home . . . All I want is to be by his side."

Is this what it means for the floodgates to open?

A part of him criticized himself for having emotions. Yet, once unleashed, he couldn't stop them flowing.

"But that's irresponsible. I have a job. There are so many cats that need care at the rescue center and a mountain of tasks that need to be completed. Putting all that aside to run home to my cat is not something a responsible person would do. Take a few days off? For my cat? Neglect work and go home because my cat is an important member of my family? Dr. Kokoro, please tell me something. If it were a human family member, it'd be acceptable, but why not for a cat? What's important is different for each person. It might not matter to others, but my cat is important to me."

But he knew better. He had common sense. That was why he couldn't act on his impulse. He'd empathize if someone around him did the same thing, but he'd also offer a gentle word of caution. It was just how he was.

All animal lovers have trodden this familiar path: dealing with compromises and conflicts that can't be discussed. *That's all it is.* He urged himself to keep it under control. But keeping a lid on one's heart was agonizing. Tomoya clutched his chest. He was in anguish; it truly felt like he might explode from the inside.

"I have no idea what will happen when. Even if I threw everything aside today, what about tomorrow? What if we spend tomorrow together, but he dies the next day? Then, everything I've done would be pointless. I don't want to live a life dragged around by a cat. No matter how important he is to me, I have to draw a line. That's why I deliberately make plans, come home as late as possible, visit my parents, and waste as much time as I can. That's how I've been convincing myself that I'm fine. But even when I do foolish things like that, I can't help but feel terrified every time I go home. What if today is the day I find Nikké dead?"

He didn't know when he started to tremble so much or to cry. Tears had filled his eyes, clouding his vision. They fell in heavy droplets as he gazed down at his clenched fists.

"I feel a wave of dread wash over me when I find Nikké motionless at home. *My cat is dead.* Then I'm relieved when I discover he's still warm. *My cat is alive.* I want to be with him, but, Dr. Kokoro, I, I . . ." Tomoya realized he should hold back.

Though Nikké seemed unresponsive, it was clear he was still listening. *It was too pitiful that his owner felt this way,* he must have been thinking.

Tomoya looked up at Dr. Suda, who remained silent. He offered neither encouragement nor blame. Swallowing his sobs, Tomoya finally released what he had been holding in.

"I want Nikké to pass away while I'm here, to pass away by my side. I can't bear the thought of him dying alone. I don't want him to die feeling lonely while I'm away."

He could no longer keep it in. Overcome by a surge of emotions, Tomoya wept and wept, his entire body shuddering.

After a while, he gradually regained his composure. Head bowed, he wiped his wet cheeks and snot-streaked face. Dr. Suda handed him a tissue.

"Thank you," he mumbled as he cleaned his face. It was the first time he had cried so hard. He was embarrassed by his display of emotion.

"I'm sure there are many things stressing you. Sometimes, it's helpful to let it all out like that. When a human is overwhelmed, it's the pet that suffers the consequences," Dr. Suda said gently.

Many might be exasperated at the sight of a grown man breaking down, but Dr. Suda showed no such reaction, nor did he show any pity. He treated man and beast alike—with neither too much empathy nor disregard.

Tomoya thought Dr. Suda was an old-fashioned type, a vet who relied on experience for his diagnoses. The latest advancements in modern veterinary science and research had likely passed him by. Yet, he had been the one who had opened his doors in the dead of night. He worked himself to the bone for the animals. Above anything, his love for them was palpable.

He wondered if he could ever become like him.

"Dr. Kokoro, I'm sorry you had to see me in this pathetic state."

"Not to worry. Listening is about all I can do."

"Just having you listen has been an enormous relief. I've been having these cruel thoughts, even though I work with animals. I feel terrible for it, especially toward Nikké. I wish I could be composed and kind like you."

"You can think whatever you want in your head. Good or bad, the fact that you're thinking things through is what counts. It's much better than not think-ing at all, like me."

Dr. Suda smiled, stroking the still-sleeping Nikké.

"I don't understand the hearts of animals or humans. It's ironic that my name, Kokoro, means 'heart.'"

It was the first time Tomoya had heard Dr. Suda speak about himself, and the rare occurrence surprised him. Although he didn't perceive any emotion in Dr. Suda's words, he wondered if a complicated past lay hidden beneath the surface. Dr. Suda's face remained inscrutable as always.

Dr. Suda placed his fingertips on Nikke's eyes and lifted the lids.

"No response at all. It's as if his consciousness departed him. He was fine this morning, right? I wonder if something changed or if there was a trigger for this."

The mention of a "trigger" sparked a thought in Tomoya.

"That clinic!"

"Which clinic are you referring to? What kind of treatment did they provide?"

"No, it's not a veterinary clinic. I mean Nakagyō Kokoro Clinic for the Soul, a peculiar mental health facility nearby. Since I visited that place, Nikké has been more alert around me. I initially thought it was a coincidence."

He thought back to the exchange at the clinic. What had the doctor and nurse said?

Something about a cat on standby? The cat not being effective? They said to take the cat I have at home, and, if that didn't work, to come back to the clinic, but they doubted I'd need to return?

"If Nikké doesn't work . . ." he mumbled. *If I go back to the clinic, will he wake up?*

He knew it was absurd. He wasn't one to believe in fantastical notions.

Still, if there was even a slim chance, he had to go.

Although it was daytime, the alley remained dark. The building at its far end was indeed identical to the one where Nikké had been trapped.

He didn't believe in mysterious phenomena, but when he opened the door to the clinic and saw the nurse at the reception window, he recognized there were many enigmas in the world still unknown to him.

This woman.

He'd met her a few times at Suda Animal Hospital.

She was the owner of the calico that was rescued along-side Nikké.

The nurse gave Tomoya a fleeting glance and let out a coquettish sigh.

"Mr. Kajiwara, you must have run out of your pre-scribed cat."

I'm sure it's her. Though not flashy, she had the air of an entertainer, and her eyes carried a hint of sorrow. He had exchanged only a few words with her two or three times in the vet's waiting room, but even then, he had felt a jolt when he saw her.

What's she doing here?

As he stood in a daze, the nurse called out to him, "Mr. Kajiwara?"

"So, like I said before, I think we've . . ."

He couldn't bring himself to say *we've met before.*

What is this? Are you hitting on me? He blushed at the memory of the nurse's mocking laugh.

". . . Nothing. Again, I don't have an appointment, but is that okay?"

"The doctor has been expecting you, Mr. Kajiwara. But personally, I hoped you wouldn't come back. That man is a fool, so he'll chuckle and prescribe you an ef-fective cat. After giving up on himself, that is."

The nurse looked a bit sad and even pained. Tomoya was confused by the nurse's remark when she said she had hoped he "wouldn't come back."

"If this isn't a good time, I can always come back a different day . . ."

"That chair is reserved for patients with appointments. Please take a seat and wait."

". . . All right."

Tomoya did as he was told. *What's with this place?* Everything about this clinic was odd, but the feeling of waiting to see the doctor was the same as anywhere else: a slight anxiety mixed with a glimmer of hope that maybe this time, they could help in some way. The fact that he found it unsettling not to have a pet carrier on his lap demonstrated how accustomed he was to visiting the vet.

"Mr. Kajiwara, please come in," called a voice from the examination room.

Tomoya was greeted by a smiling doctor in a lab coat. He took a seat, and they faced each other at a close distance.

"Hello, Mr. Kajiwara. How are you? Are you feeling better?"

Tomoya took a long, hard look at the smiling doctor.

He had sensed something unusual the other day, too. What could it be? It felt as though he was observing himself. He felt dizzy.

"Excuse me, doctor?"

"Yes?"

"Have we met before?"

Tomoya knew it was absurd, but it felt as if he were talking to his reflection in the mirror. It was almost scary.

As Tomoya's face tensed up, the doctor burst into bright laughter.

"A pickup line, Mr. Kajiwara? Seriously, please refrain from flirting during a medical exam."

Tomoya's face flushed crimson. He attempted to stand up, but he was so agitated that he struggled to push the chair back smoothly.

"I'm leaving."

"Oh, no, no, no. I was just joking. Please don't take me seriously."

Tomoya reluctantly sat back down. Both the doctor and the nurse were not taking this seriously. He was known to be mild mannered, but he couldn't help but show his displeasure on his face. Yet the doctor and nurse acted as if nothing was wrong.

"It doesn't matter how you meet, whether it's through

a pickup line or if you're set up on a date, even though humans like to imbue encounters with meaning. They enjoy discussing fate and once-in-a-lifetime moments, but these are narratives created after the fact. A simple coincidence or whim on that day, at that moment—that's all it takes. After all, there are plenty of people and cats in this world. Really, there are. Mr. Kajiwara, there really are a ton."

Tomoya began to feel unsettled by this doctor's ongoing claim that he had been flirting.

"What do you mean?" he asked.

"I want you to figure out the meaning for yourself. So, how did it go? Do you feel like you got everything off your chest and felt heard?"

"*What?*" Tomoya felt exhausted from how much the conversation jumped from topic to topic.

The doctor, however, was grinning from ear to ear.

"You said you've been absent-minded and that you are making mistakes. Is that still the case? Did talking about it make you feel better?"

". . . Do you mean at Dr. Kokoro's?"

"Ultimately, it's not me who has healed you but you and the people around you. I'm so glad you're feeling better. It's about time the eternally sleeping cat moved on, don't you think?"

"How do you know about my cat?"

Nikké, still in a deep sleep, had been left in the care of Suda Animal Hospital. Tomoya had work tomorrow. Should he leave Nikké so he could be closely observed by Dr. Suda, or should he bring him home and spend his days worrying again? He was afraid he'd regret whichever option he chose.

This doctor knew about Nikké and was also aware of Dr. Suda. The nurse was likely the same woman he'd seen come and go from the vet. They shared a close relationship with Suda Animal Hospital. It couldn't be a coincidence that he'd come here. Something had drawn him in. Tomoya tried to calm himself down.

"My cat has been in a sort of semicomatose state for almost a year, and we don't know why. But since I've come here, he's begun to wake up. Then, he lost consciousness again. If you have any insights that might help, please tell me. How can my cat capture his lively spirit again?"

"Your cat will not wake up again," the doctor said with a faint smile. "It's his time."

A silence descended. Tomoya could hear the beating of his own heart. In that instant, he realized he had the answer. Keeping his gaze fixed on the doctor, he declared, "If that's the case, I'll stay by his side."

"You can't do that." The doctor shook his head. "Everyone is alone when they die. Just as you can't choose the moment you meet someone, you also can't choose the moment you die—people, animals, everyone. Please don't cling to your need to avoid regret."

"But my cat has gone through a lot of hardship. I don't want him to feel alone when he dies."

"If that's the case, let me share something that might ease your mind." The doctor erupted in laughter, his face breaking into a broad smile that swept away all prior solemnity. "Cats are much stronger than you realize. When they close their eyes, they enter a realm of delightful fantasies. Even if they're completely alone, cats possess the strength to pass away while dreaming of happy things. After all, cats can solve all problems. Well, maybe 'all' is a bit of an overstatement. Lately, I find myself in hot water when I make exaggerated claims."

As Tomoya sat in confusion, the doctor kept nodding as though his words were entirely logical.

"I actually wanted to prescribe you a very effective,

cute cat to help remind you of the joy of spending time with cats. I thought it would be good for you to have a cheerful one that would make you laugh. But I'm glad to hear your cat at home seemed to have a little bit of effectiveness left." He paused and steepled his fingers. "Hmm, so how are you feeling? Since your symptoms are improving, what do you think about trying a different cat next?"

"*No way!*" The curtains in the back whipped apart, revealing the nurse, who stood there, tall and imposing. "Why do you give up so easily, doctor? Why not be more persistent, throw a fit, and stand your ground? Fight for your owner's attention! Fight for your life! You can do that, can't you? You're still here, aren't you?"

When she was done, she yanked the curtains closed.

It all took place in the blink of an eye.

As Tomoya and the doctor sat frozen in place, the curtains parted again. The nurse had reappeared, anger in her eyes.

"Aren't you a man? If you have balls, show some guts!" And then, the curtains swiftly shut again.

The two of them stared silently at the curtains, waiting for them to part again. Eventually, the doctor swiveled his chair around to face Tomoya.

"Well, that was quite the jab. She must have had a cup of extra-strong catnip tea if she's asking if I have balls . . ."

"Uh, did she? I didn't quite hear," Tomoya stammered, burying his face in his hands, trying not to crack up. He had actually heard everything clearly, but he hesitated to burst out laughing since the nurse was likely listening.

"Balls," the doctor said thoughtfully. "Guts. Man, Chitose doesn't pull any punches. It always feels like I'm getting a good smack on the head. Wakes me right up, though, so I appreciate it."

"She's . . . bold."

Tomoya couldn't think of any other word he could say out loud without landing himself in trouble. Perfect expressions like "willful" or "arrogant" seemed likely to earn him a whack on the head, too.

"She's like a younger sister to me," the doctor said with a carefree laugh. "We've known each other for a long time. By fate, we'd become neighbors for a while. There were many of us in the group, but she's the only one who stuck by me, never giving up until the very end. She's kind and strong, and she's also beautiful."

The doctor glanced at the curtains. Although it had initially looked like the doctor was receiving a one-sided scolding, it seemed like the two had a strong bond. The mention of "younger sister" made Tomoya think of his own.

"Now, what should we do, Mr. Kajiwara?"

"Huh?"

"There are many cats in this world, and every cat is just a cat. But when you care for one, that cat becomes more than 'just a cat.' It becomes therapeutic. When you're having a hard time or you see difficulties on the horizon, you don't have to tough it out. Getting treatment early can prevent things from getting worse. That's not a bad thing at all."

The doctor smiled.

I've seen that face somewhere.

The affable yet teasing irreverence. He *knew* he recognized that face, but not that smile. The reflection he usually saw in the mirror was far more somber.

Reflection in the mirror?

Tomoya shook his head. *Impossible. What am I thinking?* It seemed he had been swept up in the strange atmosphere of this clinic. This was a mental health clinic. Its methods and the doctor were unconventional, but they healed the soul's aches. He'd come here by his own choosing, for his own benefit, and opened the door himself.

"What would you like to do? Should we prescribe you a cat?"

The doctor giggled.

Tomoya furrowed his brow. As always, the doctor's smile was flippant.

——— · ———

When he emerged from the examination room, all he saw was the empty seat.

Tomoya hovered for a moment. Ultimately, he had received no treatment. All he had was a pointless conversation with a weirdo doctor. He had wasted his time here while Nikké was quietly waiting for him at Suda Animal Hospital.

But strangely, he felt better—refreshed, even.

"Mr. Kajiwara?"

A pale hand beckoned to him from the reception. The nurse was looking at him from the window with a serious expression.

She was indeed beautiful, but when he recalled what she had said to the doctor earlier, he nearly burst into laughter.

"The doctor said to let any patients with appointments come in. Has anyone shown up?"

The nurse sighed.

"Ms. Torii has been giving us a hard time. Just when we think she's finally coming, she vanishes again. She's long finished her cat prescription, but she's simply abandoned her treatment. In any case, we can't close this place yet. I need the doctor to hold on until all the patients with appointments are healed." She suddenly turned to Tomoya with a stern glare. "Mr. Kajiwara?"

"Y-yes?"

"He can be reckless when it comes to himself, so please take good care of him, okay? I'm counting on you."

". . . All right."

He wasn't quite sure why he was being scolded. He was really not very fond of this woman. He turned his back to the reception window when a surprisingly gentle voice reached his ears.

"When it's time for your cat to go far away, he will always remember the joyful times he spent with you."

Tomoya turned around and saw the nurse was smiling.

"I, too, passed away alone, when no one was around. Even so, it wasn't cold, and it wasn't lonely. I stayed with my special person until the very end and was happy until it was time for me to go. That's what it means for a cat to love a person. If you ever meet my special person, please pass that on. Now, take care."

Then, the nurse dropped her gaze as if she hadn't said anything.

The doctor and nurse were both peculiar people and Tomoya didn't understand if she was talking about someone else or herself. *Or both?* He slipped quietly through the metal door and left.

When he had rescued Nikké and the others, the fifth floor had been vacant except for this unit. Now, it seemed the unit at the end of the hall was occupied, and that alone was enough to reassure him that he was indeed in the real world.

Will I ever come here again? He might if those around him encouraged him to. He was grateful for those who cared about him, and he hoped not to worry them anymore.

So I probably won't come here again.

As Tomoya was hauling around a mountain of freshly laundered blankets and cat beds, he spotted the boy who had adopted Wighead standing in the entrance hall. He and his mother were gazing intently at a sign for a workshop for children.

The mother noticed Tomoya first.

"Look, Ko, it's the deputy director."

The boy ran over to Tomoya. Tomoya set down the load he was carrying and crouched.

"Hey, sonny. You're here for our workshop?"

"Yeah. I'm going to become a cat doctor when I grow up. And I drew a picture of Met and Met's friend. You want to see?" The boy's words came tumbling out.

Tomoya didn't quite understand what he said and looked to his mother for help.

"He's talking about our cat. He thought 'Helmet' was too hard to say, so he decided to name him 'Met.' Ko, why don't you show the deputy director your picture of Met?"

"Okay!" The boy spread out the drawing paper in his hands. "This is my Met."

On the paper was a dynamic crayon drawing of . . . something. Perhaps the messy black-and-white blob was Met, formerly known as Wighead. It had what could be triangular ears and whiskers. There was also maybe a person and something resembling many-paneled curtains that surrounded Met. The boy pointed at his drawing.

"This is me. This is Mom. This is Met, and this is his friend."

From the ears and whiskers, it was just barely clear they were cats. The drawing showed two cats accompanied by the boy and his mother. Everyone in the picture had bright, joyful eyes that made you want to smile just by looking at them.

"So that's Met's friend, huh?" Still crouching down, he asked the mother, "Did you adopt another cat?"

"Oh, no! I have my hands full with Met and this child. Ko, that black cat is the deputy director's cat, right?"

The boy nodded vigorously.

"Yeah. Exactly. The black one's your cat. He's best friends with Met." He thrust his drawing out toward Tomoya again. The black-and-white blob of crayon was Met. The black smear next to it was Nikké. He was also smiling.

"I see! You drew my cat, too. Thank you."

"He's in a climbing contest with Met. Right, Mom? It's very cool."

"You're right." The mother gave Tomoya a wry smile. "Met likes to claw up curtains and wallpaper, leaving everything tattered. Cats can be even more mischievous than kids. Is it quite the scene at your home, too?"

"At my home . . ."

It seemed that the many-paneled curtains were regular curtains that had been ripped. Tomoya gazed at the smiling black cat in the picture. His narrowed, cheerful eyes resembled those of Nikké, who was presently still sound asleep. Tomoya resolved not to let his worries lead him on unnecessary detours home. He would continue to work with his usual diligence and look forward to going home. After all, as any cat owner would understand, his cat was waiting for him.

"Yes, that's true. My cat is quite the troublemaker, too. My cat also likes to scale curtains, walls, and just about anything to climb up pretty high. He'd definitely give Met a run for his money in a climbing contest."

"Yeah! It's a race!"

The boy laughed, then took his mother's hand and headed into the workshop.

As Tomoya watched the backs of mother and son, he felt a kind of invisible bond or destiny. Since the visit to the clinic, Nikké's full-moon eyes had remained closed. After checking to ensure there was a slight decrease in the amount of food and water and that the litter box was being used, Tomoya would brush Nikké's unmoving body. He'd trim his claws and hold him tight. Cats smelled warm and pleasant. When he sank his nose into the back of Nikké's neck, he could smell sunshine.

Nikké no longer climbed to high places. He could no longer play with other cats. He didn't stretch nor stare fixedly at one spot.

Even so, Tomoya wanted Nikké, for as long as possible, to cling on—to him.

He gathered up the blankets and cat beds and headed to the back of the facility. On his way, he ran into Madoka, who was preparing for the workshop.

"Tomoya, did you see? That boy's here to take the workshop."

"Yeah, I did. It seems like his interests are growing. I hope he enjoys the workshop. Have a pawsitively fun and purrfectly lively class."

As he began to head toward the storage, he noticed Madoka staring at him with a look of astonishment on her face.

"What's wrong?"

"Oh no! Tomoya! You're not better at all. If anything, you've become weird. You were not someone who'd say 'pawsitively' or 'purrfectly' anything."

"Huh? That's totally fine, isn't it?"

"No, it's not fine at all. It's completely out of character. Mr. Ōta! Tomoya is still sick. He's still troubled."

Summoned by Madoka, Mr. Ōta came over.

"What's going on?"

"Tomoya's saying things like 'pawsitively fun' and 'purrfectly lively'!"

"Oh, dear . . . maybe he's overtired?"

Tomoya left the joking duo behind as he lugged his load. He truly had a mountain of tasks to complete. He planned to tidy up efficiently, work as hard as possible, and return home to his beloved cat.

———

As usual, Nikké's limbs hung loosely, yet his tail swayed gently. He always appeared to be dreaming enjoyable dreams. Now, Tomoya could confidently believe that really was the case.

———

A noise was coming from next door again.

Akira Shiina turned off the TV and pressed his ear against the door from inside his unit. He heard the metallic clanging sound of a door opening and closing.

There were footsteps down the hallway. It seemed like someone had just left.

He quietly turned the doorknob and peeked through the crack of the door. He could just make out a figure in the dimly lit hallway; it headed toward the staircase and disappeared from sight. *Hmm. Looks like a young boy,* he thought.

He closed the door silently and let out a deep sigh. Just as he'd thought, someone had indeed settled in next door.

Or something has.

Shiina slumped down on the spot. *Business is good,* he thought. His biological age was twenty-something. Sure, he faced a few challenges in his personal life, but they weren't anything he couldn't overcome with his determination and grit.

But it seemed the magnets were powerless against eerie, unnatural phenomena. The influx of people, young and old, visiting the neighboring space remained steady. What was genuinely frustrating was that reaching out to the building's owner and management didn't solve the issue. Just the other day, he and a representative from building management visited the next-door unit and found it completely vacant—not even a mouse stirred, let alone a cat.

"Damn it. At this point, I don't care who it is; I'm going to catch anyone who comes here. I'll make them spill the beans. Or, like that time with that old man, I'll go inside with them."

He had once pulled open the absurdly heavy door and peeked inside. He was truly stunned. The interior of the unit looked different from when he'd last seen it. For just an instant, he saw something resembling a reception window at a clinic.

What was this setup? He couldn't completely disregard the possibility that it was a large-scale scam. His irritation made him crave a cigarette, but he shook his head. He had quit smoking.

Out of nowhere, he heard a sound. A feeble voice. A meowing cat. And not just one cat.

"I knew it. I don't know how it's happening, but there are definitely cats next door."

I'll get them next time.

Shiina made up his mind. The next time an opportunity arose, he was going to bust in next door and reveal their identities. He didn't care, even if they were spirits or two-tailed monster cats.

In preparation for that moment, he swapped the magnetic necklace he was wearing for the highest-grade one. He needed to ensure that he was always harnessing the maximum magnetic power.

"All right! If this helps get rid of the strange thing next door, it'll prove that the necklace has supernatural powers as well."

It lifted his spirits to think there might be a new selling point he could add to the product. He smiled with joy. He was ready to open the next heavy door for himself.

— · —

"Well, then."

Nikké leaned back in his chair and looked around his cramped examination room.

It was unrecognizable now. The room had previously been packed with cardboard boxes. His friends had always been around him. They played together, slept together, and occasionally quarreled within the large circular enclosure. Even when he was put back into his own cage, he had always believed that gentle hands would come to play with him again the next day.

But then he was left alone for a day. Then a second day. His memory of the end was quite blurry.

"That must have been tough. I wonder if she can be healed?" he mumbled toward the ceiling.

The curtains parted. Chitose stood with her brow furrowed.

"Dr. Nikké, we don't know when your next patient with an appointment will arrive, so please don't doze off and drool."

"I didn't doze off."

He sat up hastily and wiped his mouth. It was true that when he allowed his thoughts to drift, he quickly lost track of his surroundings. He thrust his chin forward at Chitose.

"Look. Any signs of drool left?"

"Yes, plenty. More importantly, I have something I've been meaning to ask: What was that thing the other day?"

"The other day?"

When Nikké tilted his head in confusion, Chitose's eyes turned fierce.

"You told Mr. Kajiwara that I was like a little sister to you. When it's the opposite. You're like a little brother to me."

"What?" Nikké exclaimed, his voice hysterical. "N-no way! I was born before you, Chitose!"

"Didn't you know? Once we reach a certain age, sibling roles switch. Therefore, you're my little brother now."

"No, that's stupid."

"So you need to listen to me, okay? Until your patient with an appointment is completely cured, you must cling on. You have to."

"You say that, but I'm pretty worn out."

"I'm not listening to your complaints. Wait, look!" Chitose turned her usual aloof gaze to the door. "Seems like someone's here again. Please try not to spend too much time with the new patients."

With that, she disappeared behind the curtains. Nikké smiled. The stubborn and spirited Chitose must have been doted on by her owner. That was why she was kind to people now.

"It can't be helped. If Chitose's still up for the challenge, I guess I could keep going for a bit more," he said toward the ceiling.

The ceiling was the only thing that hadn't changed. The grapevine had spread far and wide, ultimately bringing in the man Nikké had been hoping to see. His gentle hands were likely saving other cats somewhere, even at this moment. For Nikké's kin, he was an indispensable figure.

Nikké still hoped for one more person to step forward. She had visited once but had drifted away. He wished that the wandering winds would lead her back once more.

The door opened. A young man in a suit entered timidly, his face in a shroud of gloom. His eyes twitched suspiciously at first. But then he began to share his troubles.

Nikké gave him a bright smile.

"We'll prescribe you a cat. Chitose! Please bring the cat!"